DEAD RINGER

ALSO BY P MOSS

fiction

THE HOUDINI KILLER
VEGAS TABLOID
VEGAS KNOCKOUT
BLUE VEGAS

non-fiction

LIQUID VACATION

DEAD RINGER

P MOSS

Squidhat Press · Las Vegas, Nevada

Editor: Scott Dickensheets
Designer: Sue Campbell
Author Photo: Ginger Bruner

First Edition

ISBN: 978-0-9989872-2-4 (print)
ISBN: 978-0-9989872-3-1 (ebook)

Published by:

Squidhat Press
848 N. Rainbow Blvd. #889
Las Vegas, Nevada 89107

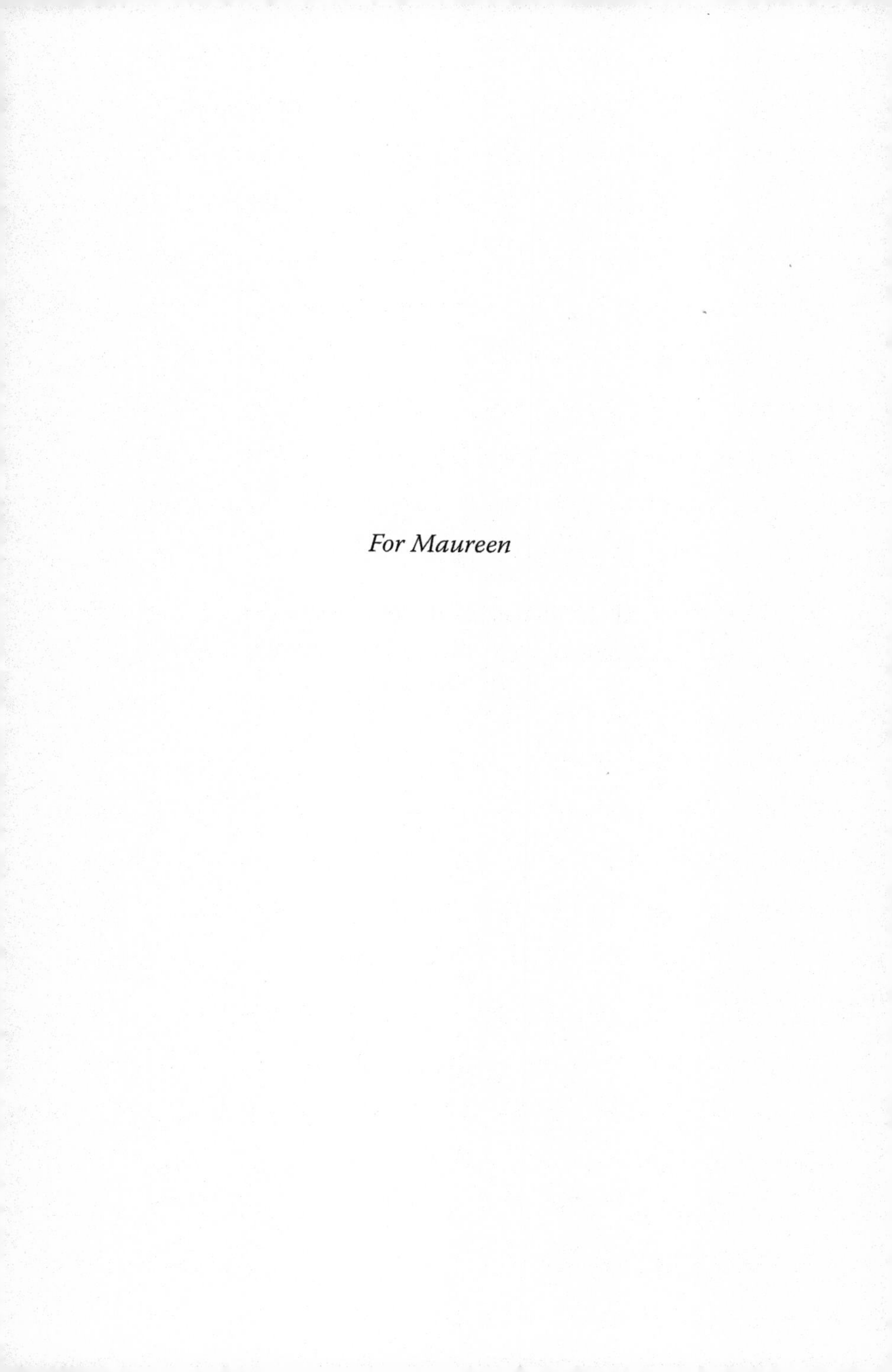

For Maureen

Although based on a 1967 event that
changed Las Vegas forever, this book
is a work of fiction

CHAPTER 1

The leggy brunette in a clinging peppermint-striped minidress belted out her best Nancy Sinatra in the lounge at Buddy Bowmar's Bowlarama, in the direction of downtown on Las Vegas Boulevard, a few blocks past where it ceased being called the Strip. Where nightly Sammy Shake cranked out Top 40 hits on his mighty Wurlitzer organ until the wee hours then loosened his tie and took requests, giving boozers the microphone to sing along. A nightly shindig that had zero to do with hitting the right notes and everything to do with having fun.

Dealers and dancers made the scene. Cabbies and trumpet players. Cocktail slingers and celebrities. Jaded night owls who welcomed an alternative to stale casino lounge combos that had snoozed through the British Invasion and emerging Haight Ashbury flower power circus. It was 1967 and not even rube tourists wanted to suffer *Satisfaction* crooned by some never-quite-made-it baritone who still oiled his hair, which made singing with Sammy at the cozy bowling alley bar the hip late-night place to be. A boozed-up Howard

Hughes knocked over glasses as he pounded a wild drum beat on his table while twin Chinese cowgirls bopped a crazy go-go two-step as Liberace and his callboy du jour clowned their way through *I Got You Babe.* But all the while Hughes's eyes were on Sunny, the leggy brunette in the clinging peppermint-striped mini-dress, as she nursed a drink at the bar waiting for another turn at the microphone.

Sunny had cashed in on Hughes's late-night generosity a few times but had never seen him extraverted like this. Had never seen him hit the liquor like this. He never even made small talk and was very businesslike about giving her the money. Wham, bam and out the door. Sex never more than an item for the sixty-one-year-old mogul to cross off his to-do list so that he could get on to something more important. Howard Hughes was one of the richest men in America, and as Sunny watched him kick up his heels, she figured that he had finally learned to enjoy his wealth. At Buddy Bowmar's Bowlarama of all places. Then moved his party somewhere more private, where it had not taken Sunny more than a moment to understand the reason for his sudden transformation from spiritless tycoon to wild party animal. Knowledge she knew would be worth a great deal of money to the right people. Knowledge she would soon take to the bank.

Sunny's legs were quickly in the air as she was tag-teamed by twin Chinese sex toys and the lanky millionaire who wore only a cowboy hat and a gun belt strapped around his skinny ass. Her mind often wandered when a tryst extended beyond the usual quick come and go, this time taking her back a few years to when she was fresh out of college and teaching fourth grade in Los Angeles, curious as to how one of the other rookie teachers could afford expensive clothes and a new convertible while she struggled to pay the rent on a studio apartment. Discovered that her co-worker flew to Las Vegas every weekend to turn tricks and soon was invited to go along, the defining moment in her life as Sunny never looked back.

Hughes jammed the barrel of his six-shooter inside her, the cold steel painful as it abraded pink inner flesh, yet she screamed with delight as that was what the man paying for this party wanted to hear. Harder and faster. Again, and again. The rougher the action the greater an actress Sunny became, making sure that those screams continued to rattle the windows as long as the meter was running.

CHAPTER 2

Moe Dalitz sat alone in the busy coffee shop picking at a plate of lox and eggs, sparring with a bit of arthritis but otherwise was in good health for a man of sixty-seven. Full head of gray hair. Coral-blue suit, white tie and diamond cufflinks. Always diamond cufflinks. He gazed out the window of the bright open room and watched guests at his Desert Inn Hotel swimming and sunning on an unseasonably warm March day, during that in-between time when gamblers recharged their batteries before hitting the casino for another shot at money that would never belong to them.

The Desert Inn was the jewel of the Las Vegas Strip, and the man in charge had come a long way since his days skiffing illegal booze across Lake Erie during Prohibition. His Mayfield Road Gang bossing the Cleveland underworld for twenty years, a good run in an industry where odds were long that a man would die in his own bed. But whether by murder, extortion or simple intimidation, Dalitz had been able to manipulate those odds in his favor until the mid-1940s when he decided to migrate west and muscle in on fresh opportunity. Put down new roots and reinvent himself in a live-and-let-live town where almost anyone could.

"It wasn't too long ago that Wilbur Clark was the one sitting here ogling the girls at the pool," Cliff Chandler said as he slid uninvited into the booth.

Dalitz choked on a cloud of Old Spice and pushed away his plate, appetite gone as he found himself seated across from the man with a salt and pepper flattop who had been annoying him for weeks.

"Sad how Clark lost this place," continued Chandler, alluding to the man who had run out of money during construction of the Desert Inn and in 1950 was bailed out by Dalitz in exchange for half interest in the property. Who fronted to the public as the gangster ran the show and skimmed the cash until Dalitz grew tired of being the power behind the throne and kicked Wilbur Clark to the curb. "But very gratifying that the same thing is about to happen to you."

Chandler, fit and approaching middle age, had one of the most recognizable faces in Las Vegas thanks to the popular Cliff Chandler Chevrolet television commercials he starred in with his bulldog Cliff Jr. And it was this local celebrity along with a squeaky-clean reputation that appealed to the Mormon church when selecting the man in the tan sports jacket and spit shined cowboy boots to establish their business interests on the Strip. Too long had the church hierarchy watched mobsters raking in the millions being made from gambling, alcohol, caffeine and all the other vices they felt traded on men's weaknesses and had finally decided it was the Lord's will that the money now go to them. The church had guaranteed a $10 million bank loan for Cliff Chandler to purchase the Desert Inn and would pave the way to expedite approval of his gaming license. The only thing wrong with the plan was that the Desert Inn was not for sale. But Cliff Chandler was a determined man who never took no for an answer.

"Last chance, Dalitz. You can do this the easy way or the hard way."

"If that's meant to be a threat, you should consider very carefully who you're talking to."

"A washed-up gangster trying to buy your way into polite society." Chandler saw Dalitz's expression tighten, pleased that he had hit a nerve. "How much did it cost to get the local bigwigs to throw you that wing ding at the Aladdin tonight? Think of how much respectability you could buy with an extra $10 million."

"Respectability? That's rich coming from a car salesman."

"Face it, Dalitz. It's a new era in Las Vegas and there's no place for you and your kind anymore. Not that there ever was."

"This town would still be a pimple on God's ass if it wasn't for men like me who were willing to put up the hard cash necessary to build something out of nothing," said Dalitz, knowing that without him, Las Vegas would still be a Mormon water stop in the middle of nowhere with chumps like Chandler kicking around in the dirt trying to shake down the Indians. "I've been telling you for over a month that I will never sell this hotel, so get your ass back to that junkyard of yours and turn back some odometers before I lose my temper."

"I'm giving you one last chance to do this the easy way."

"Go piss in your hat."

"Then prepare to be indicted by the federal government on charges of tax evasion for skimming undeclared cash from the casino. And the Gaming Commission won't wait for a jury to convict you before revoking your license to operate this place."

Murder and intimidation had gotten Dalitz through Prohibition. Shrewdness and cunning side-stepped Eliot Ness and the Kefauver Committee. Sharp lawyers and accountants had beaten back multiple tax indictments. And there was no doubt in his mind that Cliff Chandler's lame shakedown attempt would go the way of dozens of other cockroach moves he had squashed all the way back to the advent of the Tommy gun and Molotov cocktail.

"Even if there is an indictment, my lawyers will have Uncle Sam chasing his tail for years. And as far as my gaming license, I have just as much political juice as you Mormons do, and we both know that for the Gaming Commission to turn against me you would need a lot more than unfounded accusations. You'd need a witness."

"I have a witness."

Cliff Chandler gauged Dalitz's reaction but the casino boss did not flinch.

"And if you're half as smart as you think you are, you'll sell me the Desert Inn before he testifies, and they take it away from you."

CHAPTER 3

Garlands of lavender and gardenia adorned the ballroom but the prevailing aroma wafting through the black-tie gala was money. Champagne flowing freely as community leaders and celebrities kicked up their heels in honor of Moe Dalitz, the man responsible for spearheading completion of a new wing at Sunrise Hospital, a first-class medical center that several years earlier he had been instrumental in founding. Dean Martin was in top form as he good naturedly roasted the man regarded as the godfather of Las Vegas philanthropy, then as the laughs gave way to Count Basie and his orchestra, flashbulbs popped as Dalitz took his wife Averill for a spin on the dance floor.

A sexy daughter of privilege flirted with a man at the bar whose Carnaby-striped suit severely contrasted the formality of the occasion, Dom Perignon absorbing her inhibitions as she pressed close and lit his cigarette. Any other evening, this tall man with longish brown hair and a sharp jawline would not have wasted another moment before getting her out of her low-cut gown, but tonight Harry Lake's attention was focused squarely on the guest of honor who danced with his better half while at the same time exchanging furtive glances with the governor's wife. A familiar play he recognized as anything but innocent as he knew better than anyone that Dalitz got his rocks off screwing the wives of men he did business with.

Harry Lake knew all the secrets as, even at a youthful thirty-one, he was not only president of the Desert Inn but Moe Dalitz's second in command concerning all matters both on and off the books, including relaying the boss's more confidential orders so that the top banana could never be directly tied to anything illegal. Harry enjoyed the money and prestige his position afforded him though dreaded delivering bad news to the man in charge. But as he watched Dalitz soak up the spotlight knew that he had no choice but to intrude with a flash that could not wait.

Dalitz blew his top as he followed Harry into the men's room, champagne glass in his hand as he checked the stalls to make certain they were alone then shoved the white jacketed attendant out the door and locked it.

"What's so goddam urgent that you couldn't even take the time to change into a tux?"

"I just got word that the cops arrested Sid Klein for beating up a hooker. He almost killed her, and they've got him dead to rights."

"City or County?"

"County," Harry told him. "But ..."

"It's your job to take care of shit like this, Harry. Not to crash my party on a night when everybody who's anybody is here. Movie stars. Politicians. Even Trafficante and Lansky flew in from Florida to kiss my ass. Now get the fuck out of here and tell the sheriff to make Sid's pinch go away."

"The sheriff can't help with this one."

"For all the money I pay that shit kicker, he had goddam better make it go away."

"The case has already gone to the district attorney, who agreed to drop the charge if he rolls over on you." Harry lit a Lucky Strike, then looked nervously through drifting smoke. "Sid Klein is Cliff Chandler's witness."

"Sid would never rat me out. He's been with me at the D.I. since the beginning. We go fishing together and I was at his daughter's wedding."

"It's a done deal, Moe."

"Sid would *never* rat me out," argued Dalitz, as if saying it twice would make it true.

"As slot operations manager he knows about a lot of things we can't afford to have the D.A. squeeze out of him."

"If this is true, why is he still working? I saw him on the casino floor this afternoon."

"Because the D.A. is smart enough to know that he can't guarantee his safety in jail, so he wants everything to appear normal and not raise any suspicions until Sid testifies before the Gaming Commission and gives a deposition to the feds."

"So, what if he does sing? They've got no case because they can't connect me directly to the skim or anything else."

"Before I came to work for you eight years ago you were directly involved in everything, and Sid can connect you to all of it."

"This whole thing is nothing but a cheap shakedown so

those fucking Mormons can try to heist my hotel."

"Maybe it is and maybe it isn't. But we can't afford to wait and see who blinks first, because the minute Sid Klein testifies, they'll have more than enough evidence to slam the bars shut on both of us."

"I haven't held a gun in my hand since I came to Vegas, but that's not going to stop me from picking one up now and showing that rat that nobody fucks with Moe Dalitz and lives to tell about it."

Harry could always be counted upon to do whatever necessary to resolve even the stickiest situations both on and off the books, and though this often meant crossing a legal line it had never involved violence. He hated violence, feeling that no matter what the situation, there was always a better way. A smarter way. Leaving Harry unprepared for the crisis of conscience in which he was about to find himself, needing to do some fast talking to keep Dalitz from putting him behind the eight ball.

"Don't let anger cloud your judgement, Moe. You're taking this too personally."

"Of course, I'm taking it personally." Rage swelling as Dalitz gulped the remainder of his champagne then smashed the glass in the sink. "He's been a guest in my home more times than I can count, and I want the satisfaction of watching that cocksucker die."

"There are smarter ways to take care of this."

"He rats, he dies."

The venom in Dalitz's eyes told Harry it would be impossible to talk him out of killing Sid Klein.

"Then be smart, Moe. If he dies, circumstantial evidence will point directly at you. He'll be just as dead if you are a long way from Vegas when it happens."

They argued back and forth until finally Dalitz was convinced that making himself vulnerable was a sucker's play.

"All right, Harry. Make the call."

Words that placed Harry *directly* behind the eight ball. But it was not Dalitz who had put him there, it was Sid Klein, who was trying to save his ass by making them pay the price for his crime. Leaving Harry with no choice but to go against everything he believed in and make the call, as even a trusted second in command did not say no to Moe Dalitz without suffering the consequences.

"Make it happen tomorrow, Harry." Dalitz looked in the mirror and ran a wet comb through his hair, then shot his cuffs and straightened his cummerbund. "And no sneaking up behind him with two in the back of the head. I want that rat prick to see it coming."

After giving the order to murder his friend, the guest of honor rejoined the celebration as a distinguished looking man and his wife walked over and asked if they could have their picture taken with him.

Moe Dalitz smiled as if he did not have a care in the world.

"Of course, Governor."

CHAPTER 4

Dark glasses cut the glare of morning sunlight as Dalitz and his wife stood on the tarmac at McCarran Field, named for the late U.S. Senator who years earlier had pulled the strings that allowed a man with a ferocious criminal past to be granted a gaming license to operate the Desert Inn. Dalitz often enjoyed deep sea fishing on his yacht and kicking back at his villa in Acapulco, but today's hastily arranged getaway would be less exotic as he and Averill prepared to board a Pacific Air Lines puddle jumper to Palm Springs for a couple days of relaxation.

The laid-back oasis for the rich and famous was a complete one-eighty from the nonstop tempo of the Strip, and his wife enjoyed the afternoon shopping on Palm Canyon Drive while Dalitz made himself conspicuous by glad handing friends and playing gin rummy at the Ingleside Inn. But pleasurable as it was, Dalitz would much rather have been back in Las Vegas snuffing the life out of the friend he had once trusted. The friend who had so often enjoyed both his generosity and the hospitality of his home. The friend who had turned rat. A betrayal that made him long for his days in Cleveland when violence was not an urge that needed to be suppressed. When he didn't need to get on a plane to alibi himself for a hit where he would not even pull the trigger. Thought fondly of the night at the Torchlight Grill when he had excused himself after finishing his last bite of steak then stepped outside, put a bullet in the ear of Barney Boyle and was back at the table in time for cheesecake. Old news. Only a sucker lived in the past. It was now a Technicolor world and Moe Dalitz had no choice but to adapt by doing whatever necessary to protect his elite position in that world.

That evening the Dalitzes joined Dick and Pat Nixon for cocktails at the Thunderbird Country Club where they ran into fellow casino owner Charlie Taxitolo. The Las Vegas Strip was such a cash cow that competitors could afford to be friendly, but that harmony did not always extend to the wives, as Marie Taxitolo turned a cold shoulder to the group.

"Get my coat, Charlie."

"We just got here."

"I said get my coat. We're leaving."

"Why was Marie so rude?" wondered Averill Dalitz as the Taxitolos made a quick exit. "And I don't mean to be catty, but she looked awful. Pale and skinny."

"She has cancer," Pat Nixon said. "And from what I hear, she doesn't have long."

"Probably wouldn't have voted for me anyway," cracked the former vice president, already three sheets to the wind as he signaled to the waiter for another Mai Tai. "Did you hear the one about the stewardess with three tits?"

"Back up, Dick," said Dalitz.

"She used the third one for ..."

"Not that." Dalitz looked across the table at the man who seemed to always need a shave. "What you said about voting. Does that mean you're running in '68?"

"I'm not ready to announce yet, Moe, but as your friend I'm advising you to start saving your money because presidents cost a lot more than governors."

Then as the shitfaced Nixon asked if anyone had heard the one about the little old lady screwing a German Shepherd, in the desert outside Las Vegas a sheriff's deputy tossed a shovel to Sid Klein.

Klein threw it on the ground.

The deputy reached for his sidearm.

"You can kill me. But you can't make me dig my own grave."

"Put the gun away, Bill," Sheriff Ralph Lamb said to his top deputy, then leaned against the fender of his truck and looked at Klein, whose image was lit only by moonlight and the distant glow of neon. "You're right, we can't make you dig. But if you don't, I can't guarantee that your daughter and that new family of hers might not meet with an unfortunate accident."

Sid Klein picked up the shovel and began to dig. The ground was hard. Progress was slow.

"Hurry up, will ya," said the cowboy sheriff as he zipped up his jacket. "My wife is making pot roast for dinner."

"Fuck you."

"I know you don't like digging, Sid. But have some sympathy for poor Bill here, who has to put all that dirt back."

The chilling desert breeze pricked at sweat and tears as

the condemned man stepped up the pace, not so the sheriff could get home for dinner, but because the sooner he finished the sooner the torture would end. His brain exploding in an urgent kaleidoscope of emotion as the hole deepened. Thinking about the petite blonde he had beaten within an inch of her life because, shit, he couldn't even remember why he had turned her face into hamburger. Thinking about his own wife's pot roast that he would never again enjoy. About his daughter who was about to give birth to grandchild he would never bounce on his knee. He would never again taste a cold beer, go bowling or play golf. All because he had gotten himself jammed up, with the only possible way out a choice between two evils which was no choice at all. He finished digging and dropped the shovel. Took off his gold wedding band and tossed it to the sheriff.

"Please see that my wife gets this."

Ralph Lamb threw the ring into the hole, then took a .38 caliber revolver from the glove compartment of his truck.

"Moe Dalitz says goodbye."

CHAPTER 5

"Never lay points with a team that's lost two in a row," advised Harry Lake from his perch on the shoeshine chair inside Churchill Downs Race & Sports Book as he and the old man working the brushes checked out the chalkboard listing the day's basketball lines.

"I'm tellin' you, the Lakers are a sure thing," pressed the shine man, a broken-down soul whose optimism was based on the overheard kibitzing of men who drove Cadillacs and flashed fat bankrolls. "You'd be smart to get some money down."

"Is your money down?"

"Not just yet, Mr. Lake. But if business is good today you can be sure that it will be."

Sporting a wide-striped blue and red sweater over flared jeans, Harry approved the shine on his boots, climbed down from the chair and slipped the shine man $100. Then almost had his hair parted by a beer bottle that screamed past his head and smashed the picture tube of one of the two rabbit-eared TVs behind the betting counter.

"Damn it, Louie!" the sports book manager yelled at the man who had murdered his television because a missed free throw with one second left on the clock had turned a $5,500 ticket on the Milwaukee Bucks into a square of toilet paper. "Get the fuck out of here. For good this time."

"He'll be back tomorrow with a new nineteen-inch Zenith and all will be forgiven," said a sixty-something bald man in a loud golf shirt and black-rimmed glasses as Harry parked himself beside him at the end of a row of transplanted stadium seats.

"$500 says you're wrong, Mister S."

"Make it a grand," countered the older man as he scratched a stick match on the sole of his shoe and drew the flame toward the business end of a long cigar. "A storefront book doesn't pay the rent by giving a hysterectomy to a goose who lays golden eggs. Believe me, Harry. I know the psychology of dealing with bad losers from way back."

All the way back, to a small cigar store on the upper west side of Manhattan where for years Mister S ground out a good living taking bets from people who had more money than sense. But the business was not without challenges. Number one on the list, being unable to obtain a solid betting line that had not been trampled upon by the opinions of connected bookmakers. A predicament not exclusively his own and after a while Mister S saw opportunity, loaded his car and headed for a place where the weather wasn't quite so argumentative. Where for a price he called several independent New York bookmakers once a day with the opening point spreads from Churchill Downs, the most respected of Las Vegas sports books. Valuable data in great demand because it was illegal to transmit betting information, even in the newspaper, across state lines, and it wasn't long until Mister S was providing his service to a growing client list. Pocketing major cash burning up the payphone outside the no-frills strip mall sports book across from the Dunes on Las Vegas Boulevard where he had reconnected with Harry after knowing him as a kid in New York.

Harry's father was an attorney who liked betting on the Yankees and often took his young son with him to that same cigar store on the upper west side, and the boy quickly became fascinated with the colorful gamblers who hung out there. Larger than life characters who conversed in a slang all their own and would bet on absolutely anything from the World Series to which drop of rain would fall to the bottom of a windowpane first. Hooking Harry to the point where after both his parents died suddenly when he was ten, he ditched foster care and showed up at the cigar store every day after school, doing odd jobs and running errands. He was a skinny kid who got beaten up a lot until he discovered that his brain could pack a bigger wallop than his fists and developed street smarts that kept him out of trouble, eventually moving in with Mister S, who taught him manners and respect. To avoid profanity and never settle for a B on a school paper when more effort would earn an A. And then one day Harry's life changed forever when into the cigar store walked a man named Big Paulie Silver, who once a month packed a chartered United DC-8 with high rollers and took off for five days in Las Vegas.

While other kids his age played stickball and dreamed of being Joe DiMaggio, Harry became obsessed with all things Las Vegas, especially the Desert Inn where Big Paulie delivered his lambs to slaughter. The hotel provided each gambler with a free room, free food and booze, free shows and golf in exchange for giving the casino their action. For organizing these gambling junkets and collecting markers from the losers after the DC-8 landed back in New York, Big Paulie received an executive salary from the hotel plus bonuses depending upon how much money his group left behind. And on his twenty-first birthday, Harry had a window seat on a charter flight to the desert. Having been hired by Big Paulie to wrangle shuttle busses to and from McCarran Field, arrange for dinner reservations, show tickets and late-night companionship for the gamblers.

Harry got off on the twenty-four-hour action of Las Vegas and became friendly with everyone who mattered on the Strip, especially pit bosses who had the power of the pen and bellmen who could facilitate any vice. Then after two years, opportunity knocked when he was sent to collect a $60,000 marker from a dice player who dropped dead moments after handing over the cash. Harry could have said the marker had not been paid and nobody would have been the wiser, but instead he turned the money over to Moe Dalitz personally. A calculated move that paid off in spades as the casino boss took a special interest in the young man who forked over sixty large when he didn't have to. Put him to work as a graveyard blackjack dealer. Kept a close eye on him, continually testing his honesty and loyalty which led to quick advancement.

Floorman. Pit boss. Shift supervisor. Harry always went above and beyond, proving his value on every rung of the ladder until finally landing the big job as Dalitz's second in command.

"You hungry, Mister S?" Harry asked as he looked around the sports book. Fascinated, just as he had been as a young boy in the cigar store, with larger-than-life characters who conversed in gamblers' slang and would bet on absolutely anything. Even after years of enjoying the best of everything Las Vegas had to offer, this hole in the wall sports book with cigarette burns in the linoleum was the place he liked the most. The place he felt most comfortable. The place he felt most at home. "How about taking a ride over to Lew's Luncheonette?"

"Sorry, boychik," said the older man, raising his voice to be heard over the yelling in the adjoining horse room as gamblers urged their nags down the stretch at an eastern track. "I've still got some calls to make."

"Tomorrow?"

"Come by around 1:00." Mister S expelled a stream of cigar smoke, then added, "And don't forget about my thousand bucks when you see a new Zenith behind the counter."

Harry walked out into the breezy sunshine and figured that since the boss was away it was too nice an afternoon to waste by going back to work. Would ring up one of the highlighted numbers in his little black book, put the top down on his red Corvette and take a drive out to Boulder City for a burger and shake at a mom-and-pop diner he liked. He dropped a dime into the payphone, but before he could dial, Cliff Chandler snatched the receiver from his hand and hung it up.

"Killing Sid Klein isn't going to keep me from taking over the Desert Inn."

"Just because Sid didn't show up for work today doesn't mean that he's dead."

"Play dumb all you want, Lake, but Sid did a lot of talking before he disappeared. Particularly about you, and how you get to keep a thin sliver of the pie for orchestrating the skim of unreported revenue."

"Which means nothing until he says it under oath."

"You're a lawyer now?"

"I read a lot."

"You should try the *Book of Mormon*," said Chandler, noticing a pretty girl waving at Harry from a passing car.

"Careful Chandler," said Harry as he brushed back his lengthy windswept hair. "Isn't jealousy a sin?"

"Why would I ever be jealous of you?"

"Because I drink beer, screw girls and enjoy all the things that you Mormons deny yourselves. What kind of ass-backwards religion denies its followers the simple pleasures of life?"

"Don't criticize what you don't understand."

"What I understand is that some snake oil salesman named Joe Smith called himself a prophet and conned your great-great grandfather into believing that he had to live his life without enjoyment in order to get into heaven, and that even now in the space age a sheep like you is still dim-witted enough to buy that nonsense as gospel."

"You're arrogant, Lake. And just like Dalitz, you think you're above the law. But sticking with that gangster is going to leave you either dead or in prison, and even you must understand that no amount of money is worth that. So why do you remain loyal to him? No matter what he's promised you, when push comes to shove, you'll be left holding the bag. Whether it's for Sid Klein's murder, skimming or whatever else you crooks are up to, the surest bet in town is that when the law closes in, Dalitz will leave you to take the fall."

The thought of making license plates for the next twenty years would have been unsettling if there was even the slightest chance of it happening, but Harry was confident that if he stayed the course events would play out exactly as he needed them to.

"Look, Harry." Chandler's tone softened. "I just came from the district attorney who said that federal prosecutors are willing to drop all charges against you if you agree to testify against Dalitz. Plus, grant you blanket immunity for all past offenses."

"I'm pretty sure the statute of limitations has expired for that pack of baseball cards I swiped in the fourth grade."

"Let me be your friend, Harry. I can keep you out of prison."

"Any case the feds think they have would disappear if something happened to Sid Klein."

"We both know Klein is dead. And the government has a strong case with or without his testimony, so when your world comes crashing down don't forget that I offered you a chance to save yourself by doing the right thing."

"The right thing for who?"

Harry turned his back on Chandler, selected a highlighted number from his little black book and dropped his dime back into the payphone.

CHAPTER 6

Freddy fussed with a kink in his hair that would not lay quite right. Had never laid quite right since switching from Brylcreem to the dry look, but that did not slow the ginger-topped bell captain's pursuit of the curvaceous cocktail slinger he watched glide through the casino that was vibrant with early evening action.

"Thinking about asking her out?"

"Thinking about fucking her brains out," Freddy told Harry who had just walked up to the bell desk, his eyes still following the raven-haired stunner whose skimpy uniform accentuated long legs and tits like torpedoes. "But the broad wants me to spring for a steak then take her to see Bobby Darin at the Flamingo."

"Maybe she's worth it."

"Maybe if she was twins." As his target disappeared from view, the bell captain shifted gears and looked seriously at Harry. "Is Mr. Dalitz selling this place?"

"Not on your life, Freddy," assured Harry over the clamor of slot machines and enthusiastic dice players who in a few hours would be shuffling back to their rooms with pockets turned inside out. "Why would you think that?"

"Because Fat Andy from room service has a brother who works over at Cliff Chandler's car lot, and he says that clown has his advertising people working on designs for a sign that says *Cliff Chandler's Desert Inn*. Bragging about all the money he's going to make here."

"He's just blowing hot air."

"Doesn't sound like that to Fat Andy's brother." Freddy stowed the suitcase of a man who had checked out of his room but was going to gamble for a couple hours before catching a cab to the airport, then looked back at Harry. "He said that just this morning the car jockey was saying things like the casino business is just like the car business because they're both people oriented. Trust built on a handshake and bullshit like that."

"Believe me when I tell you that Moe will *never* sell the Desert Inn to Cliff Chandler."

They heard a scream. Yelling.

Harry eyeballed the commotion then shot across the casino floor toward a midget with a ferocious mustache who was jumping up and down on a blackjack table before a security guard was finally able to grab the pint-sized troublemaker and hold him under his arm like a sack of potatoes.

"He and his partner took turns distracting the dealer so they could increase their bets on winning hands, Mr. Lake. The eye in the sky caught it and called down, that's when he jumped on the table. Sorry I couldn't catch his partner before he ran out the door."

"It's a bum rap. I never seen that jerkoff before in my life."

Casino action had skidded to a halt as gamblers at surrounding tables turned their attention from cards to the midget who kicked his legs at the air, struggling to free himself from the grasp of the security guard.

"Come on, Harry. Tell this asshole to put me down."

"Take him to the machine shop."

"Don't even joke about that," cringed the midget.

"Get him out of here."

"Give me a break, for fuck sake. Didn't I hip you to that fixed race at Santa Anita last year?"

"Your sure thing finished sixth."

"It wasn't my fault the horse double crossed us. And what about the time I scored us those two broads from Texas?"

"You cashed in their plane tickets, and I had to pay their way home. There's no upside to knowing you."

"You can't do this to me! We're friends, for fuck sake!"

"Friends don't steal from friends, Hollywood. Maybe losing a couple fingers will help you understand that."

"Please, Harry," the midget begged, scared to death as he kicked furiously trying to escape. "I'll do anything you want. Anything. Just tell this big ape to put me down."

"I lost a grand at Churchill yesterday because I misjudged a situation, and I'm not going to make that mistake again," said Harry, who then told the security guard, "Introduce this thief to the band saw."

"You can't do this! Tell him to let me go!"

Convinced that the midget was about to shit his pants, Harry told the security guard to put him down. Then confiscated the handful of chips he was clutching as gamblers got back to the business of gambling as if the ballyhoo had never happened.

"That's my money, Harry. I made an honest score at the Stardust before I came over here."

The midget was a well-known scammer and thief whose street smarts were not quite enough to overcome a cut-rate IQ. Who bragged that he was an actor who had played a Munchkin in *The Wizard of Oz,* even though when that movie was released he was still in diapers. Although he did have a featured role in a porno flick that was released just the week before.

"How much did you buy in for, Hollywood?"

"$800."

"Is that what the dealer will tell me?"

"Okay, Harry. I bought in for forty bucks. That's all I got from that skirt at the Stardust. You know I'm not tall enough to dip into men's pockets where the real money is, so I gotta go after the sweater dollies who play slots till I find one rube enough to leave her purse on the floor by her chair, then when she gets distracted by three cherries or some shit, I dip into her bag for whatever I can grab. I know it ain't strictly sporting to take off a broad, but even a midget has to eat."

Harry handed him $40 worth of chips.

"Gimme the rest, Harry. I worked hard for that money."

"It's the casino's money, Hollywood. Now quit griping and tell me if you've heard anything on the street about Cliff Chandler."

"You mean like him buying this joint and kicking Dalitz to the curb like he did to Wilbur Clark?"

CHAPTER 7

Moe Dalitz made himself comfortable on the sofa in a hotel suite overlooking the magnificently groomed fairways of the Desert Inn's championship golf course, digs that Harry had redecorated to suit his bachelor pad lifestyle. Laughed as he noticed a Raymond Chandler novel on the coffee table.

"Research?"

"Make fun all you want, but you'd be surprised at the insight you can pick up from reading crime fiction," said Harry as he tightened the sash of his black silk kimono. "Want me to order up some breakfast?"

"What I want is to know what's been going on while I've been away."

Harry sank into a cushioned chair across from his boss. Lit a Lucky and tossed the match into an ashtray.

"Well?"

Harry held up his hand, indicating that he needed to wait a moment before answering. And as that moment passed, a fiery redhead wearing a slinky dress from the night before walked out of the bedroom, smiled, then let herself out.

"She's gone. Now let's have that update."

Harry again held up his hand, and almost on cue another beauty walked out of the bedroom and made her exit. Then as the door closed behind her, he told his boss that they had a problem with Chandler.

Dalitz held up *his* hand, then looked toward the bedroom. "You sure you aren't forgetting any?"

"This is serious, Moe. He cornered me at Churchill and said the feds would give me immunity if I found religion."

"Chandler's witness disappeared, and now he's grasping at straws because he's got no leverage."

"Then why is he still shooting his mouth off all over town about the big money he's going to make here? Why is he having a new sign designed for out front that says *Cliff Chandler's Desert Inn*? Why would he do any of that unless he has something up his sleeve?"

"With the ace I have up my sleeve, I can squash that cockroach whenever I want."

"Then why are you waiting? There's no percentage in it."

"Because the more you build up the ego of a prick like Chandler to think he has the upper hand, the more fun it is when you knock him down to size."

"So, this is just a game to you?" said Harry, annoyed with the man whose arrogance was hitting too close to home. "You're letting your own ego get in the way, Moe. Jeopardizing not just your own future, but mine too. You promised me five percent ownership of the D.I. and my name on the gaming license."

"A piece of the action that will make you rich."

"Except that you haven't made good on that promise, and it's been almost a year."

"You're not doing so badly."

Dalitz checked out two Rauschenberg collages and an original Lichtenstein on the wall, then got up from the sofa and took a look at Harry's alphabetized bookshelf. Flipped through his collection of jazz LPs, seeing that his protégé used the likes of Dexter Gordon to get women in the mood the way he had once used Artie Shaw and Harry James. Then looked out the window at the golf course home that James had once shared with wife Betty Grable.

"When you first came to me and handed over the sixty grand you collected from that dead junketeer, I wasn't sure if you were honest or just stupid. Or if maybe you were up to something else. So, for years I put you to the test again and again until finally I got the answer."

"Which is?"

"You're greedy."

"I'm ambitious."

"A man who is up to something hides his greed, but you don't hide anything from me and that's why I trust you."

"Then trust me when I tell you that Chandler is dangerous."

"He's a schmuck."

"He's got the ear of both the district attorney and the feds."

"Are you saying we should take care of him?"

"By playing that ace, or are you thinking of something more permanent? Because I'm shouldering enough guilt about the line you made me cross with Sid Klein and I won't do it again."

"You'll do whatever the fuck I tell you to do." The *or else* was implied as Dalitz let the threat sink in. Then changed direction. "Look, Harry. There's no sense in us arguing. You're smart, loyal and I appreciate everything you do. But I've been in this business a lot longer and you need to understand that I know what I'm doing. So just keep doing what I tell you and one day soon you will own a piece of this hotel."

"Neither of us will own this hotel if you don't start taking Chandler seriously."

"He's a putz."

"This isn't a game to me, Moe. You need to stop being so cocky and listen when I tell you that he is a lot smarter than you think."

"And you need to watch your tone and remember who you work for."

Harry was not likely to forget, or forget that in order to get what he wanted out of the Desert Inn he would need to cross whatever line Dalitz threw down. But was it worth it? His conscience said no. His ambition argued otherwise.

"What if Chandler makes a move we're not ready for? We need to know what he's up to."

The phone rang. Harry answered and listened a moment, then handed it to Dalitz who listened a moment then hung up.

"We're about to find out."

CHAPTER 8

"Don't barge into my office and give me a sermon about some squeaky-clean version of progress when all you're trying to do is muscle in on my action," Dalitz told Vernon White, a special emissary dispatched by the Quorum of the Twelve Apostles to oversee expansion of the Mormon church's economic footprint in Las Vegas.

"That progress is the Lord's vision."

"Vision, my ass. You Mormons are so short-sighted you'd step over a dime to snatch a nickel," Dalitz said to White, who along with Cliff Chandler were seated in green leather chairs on the other side of his expansive horseshoe-shaped desk. "You're here because this flunky car salesman of yours couldn't get the job done and called in the cavalry to help him heist my hotel."

"A hotel that you, if I may be permitted to borrow from the vernacular, heisted from the original owner," replied Vernon White, fifty years old with nary a touch of gray in hair that was combed perfectly into place. Tortoise shell glasses magnifying dark eyes and an expensively tailored suit giving him an air of conservative refinement. “Mr. Clark’s fall from grace is a cautionary tale you would be wise to heed by accepting Brother Cliff’s generous offer.”

“This cockroach has a better chance of growing tits and winning Miss America than he has of ever owning this hotel.”

“I *will* own the Desert Inn, you cheap gangster.”

“That’s enough, Cliff,” White censured sharply.

Vernon White was indeed a special emissary of the Mormon church, though the term fixer would more appropriately describe the man who a decade earlier had gained favor among the hierarchy by getting one of their chosen few out of a jam involving young boys that would have rocked the religion to its very foundation. Time and again proving himself invaluable to the point where the Twelve Apostles turned a blind eye to his often-unspeakable methods, as long as the desired result was achieved. And White never failed to deliver. His current mission to, by any means necessary, remove Moe Dalitz as the primary obstacle to the church’s pursuit of casino riches.

“The Lord has envisioned Las Vegas as a first-class city with a symphony, an opera house and fine art museums. Where Nevada Southern can evolve into a nationally respected university. Where decent families prosper, and children are not subjected to billboards and television commercials promoting sins of greed and sins of the flesh.” White’s words were crisp and precise. “A vision of wholesome abundance that will not include you, Morris, as God has determined that rightful ownership of the Desert Inn be bestowed upon Brother Cliff, who will use its bounty to bless the community.”

"Tell your god that I've singlehandedly done more for this community than all you fucking Mormons have in the last century and a half. I built a hospital, a convention center and work has already begun on the Las Vegas Country Club." Dalitz looked around his well-appointed office at framed photographs of himself with Sammy, Sinatra and a dozen other legendary headliners. Proclamations of appreciation from countless charities and civic organizations. "Not only am I a philanthropist, but this hotel provides hundreds of good-paying jobs that give families in this town a high quality of life. So why try to muscle in on me? Why not the real gangsters over at the Flamingo or the Sands? Or Caesars, for chrissakes. When that place opened last year, not only didn't they try to conceal their mob ties, they threw a party to celebrate them."

"Those properties will become easier for us to acquire following a show of strength by deposing the great Moe Dalitz." Even seated, White's perfect posture projected the self-assurance of a man who never failed to get what he wanted. "That is why it's important for us to, as you so graphically put it, muscle in on the Desert Inn first."

"You're pissing up a rope."

With no children to tie them down, Vernon White and his wife had relocated from Provo, Utah to a quiet tree-lined street west of downtown Las Vegas where he embraced the challenge of shepherding the Mormon church's vision of progress into reality. But he was not a patient man.

"The time has come to stop sparring, Morris. Either accept Brother Cliff's offer or I shall be left with no alternative but to make it known to your society friends that you have used money illegally skimmed from the Desert Inn to purchase your veneer of respectability."

"You can't prove that."

"Men of lofty position will ostracize you at the mere hint of scandal. Then distance themselves further by utilizing influence over the Nevada Gaming Commission that will undoubtedly lead to revocation of your license and a probable federal tax indictment."

"Don't threaten me, White."

"On the contrary, Morris. I am only pointing out that it would be in your best interest to retire from the casino business."

"And don't try to tell me what's in my best interest, you self-righteous prick, because beneath *your* veneer of respectability is nothing but a cheap racketeer. The whole Mormon religion is nothing but a fucking racket."

"Look in the mirror."

"A lot of people win in my casino every day. As opposed to you Mormons who extort money and sweat from your suckers without giving them anything in return but false hope."

"I did not come here to listen to an ignorant assessment of my faith."

"There's the door."

"It's time for you to make a decision, Morris. Either accept Brother Cliff's generous offer or suffer consequences that will inevitably leave you disgraced and in prison."

"I worked seventeen years building the Desert Inn into a world class resort, and you are out of your fucking mind if you think I'm just going to quit and walk away."

"Accepting a $10 million severance is hardly the same as quitting."

"Don't shit on my desk and tell me it's a Baby Ruth. You have no idea what I'm capable of doing to protect what belongs to me."

CHAPTER 9

Harry knew everybody on the Strip and everybody on the Strip knew him, but as the unenthused bartender slid him another beer at this out of the way saloon in North Las Vegas the odds were a million to one that he would run into a familiar face. A blue-collar joint that had fallen on hard times since the new highway robbed it of passing automobile traffic. No TV. Broken jukebox. Not a word of conversation in the air as there were only three other customers at the bar and two of them were asleep. A perfect place for Harry to be alone with his thoughts as, for the past hour, he had struggled with lingering guilt over the part he had played in a cold-blooded murder. He hadn't fingered Sid Klein. He had not pulled the trigger. All he had done was follow the order of his boss to make the call that set the execution in motion. An execution that would have taken place whether he had made the call or not, but that did not change the fact that he was complicit in a man's death.

Harry crushed his cigarette out in a full ashtray, thinking about how Moe Dalitz was so greedy that too much would never be enough. And how, contrary to his boss's conclusion after eight years of continually putting him to the test, he was not. But he did have a plan. An ambitious plan that went far beyond the points he had been promised in the Desert Inn. A plan that murder had caused to take an ugly turn. He had crossed a line and was battling it out with his conscience trying to decide whether or not he would allow himself to cross other lines that Dalitz, once he realized that Cliff Chandler was indeed a formidable enemy, would surely put before him.

"Money or a woman?"

Harry looked at a grizzled old man in a beat-up denim jacket who nursed a beer at the end of the bar.

"What do you mean?"

"My name don't have to be Einstein to figure that a duded up fella like you come in here to look down your nose at those of us less fortunate so you can maybe feel like your own problems ain't so bad."

"You don't know anything about me."

"I know I could live for a month on what you paid for that necktie."

Harry nodded toward the pool table.

"Shoot some stick?"

"Nothin' else to do."

As Harry reached into his pocket for a quarter, the old man nudged him out of the way and deposited a coin in the slot.

"Don't need your charity, kid."

"Don't call me kid. My name's Harry."

"Digger. Play for a beer?"

Digger racked. Harry broke and sank three balls, but never

shot again as the old man ran the table then asked if he wanted a rematch.

"Haven't you ever figured out that when you hustle someone, you're supposed to let them win the first game?"

"You got nothin' I want except that beer you owe me."

They went back to the bar and Harry ordered two cold ones.

"So, which is it, kid? Money or a woman?"

"Neither."

"The law?"

"Let's talk about something else."

"Sure, kid. Soon as you tell me what's weighing so heavy you come in here tryin' to escape it."

"Why are you so interested?"

"Like I told you before. Nothin' else to do."

"If you must know, I'm trying to figure out how far I'm willing to go to get something I want."

"How bad you want it?"

"Bad."

"Then take some advice from a man who wakes up every morning regretting the day I didn't stand up and fight for something *I* wanted bad."

"You don't strike me as a man who would back down from anything."

"Didn't back down. Not exactly, anyway. More like waited for another chance when the odds might not be so stacked against me."

"Smart move."

"Seemed so at the time, but I never got another chance."

"One way or another, there's always another chance."

"Keep thinkin' like that and you'll end up drinkin' your days away in a shithole like this." Digger took a sip of beer then looked Harry dead in the eye. "But a fancy fella like you don't think that's possible, do you?

"No, I don't."

"Then you better hope you have the balls to do whatever it takes to get whatever it is you want so bad."

"What if the price is too high?"

"If you gotta ask that question you don't want it bad enough. You gotta dig deep and do *whatever* it takes. Elsewise, you'll regret it till the day you fall over dead."

"Harry Lake!"

Harry knew the voice. A cocky blackjack dealer he had recently fired.

"I made a wrong turn coming back from Mount Charleston and figured I'd stop for a brewski and see how the other half lives," he laughed as he checked out the two decaying men sleeping at the decaying bar. "And no hard feelings about the job because I'm over at the Trop now. Much better place to work than the D.I."

"Ten to one they're not as happy about it as you are," said Harry, who then stood up and faced the old man. "I've enjoyed talking with you, Digger. And if I get what I want I'll come back and give you that rematch."

"Don't forget, kid. Do whatever it takes."

They clinked gasses and Harry drained his beer. Slid a $20 bill onto the rail.

"Thanks, mister!" brightened the bartender as he scooped up the gratuity. "Must be my lucky day."

"Don't be so sure."

"Are you kidding? The last time a $20 tip made its way across this bar was never."

Harry looked at his former employee trying to kick music out of a broken jukebox. Then back to the bartender.

"A few minutes ago, if you would have bet that twenty at a million to one odds, how much money would you have?"

CHAPTER 10

"Good afternoon, Morris," said a cheery Vernon White, as he and Chandler walked out of the Desert Inn coffee shop. "We were just talking about you."

"Whatever move you amateurs are getting ready to make, it won't work," Dalitz shot back, having observed them eating with two men in off the rack suits.

"Maybe you didn't notice who we were having lunch with," said Chandler.

"You think bringing a fed into my hotel is going to scare me, cockroach?" snapped Dalitz, having recognized one of the men as the special agent in charge of the Las Vegas field office of the FBI.

"You might find the other gentleman more intimidating," said White. "He is a forensic accountant, whose job it is to examine the books of a suspect business with far more scrutiny than a regular audit, digging deep to investigate every aspect of the operation from top to bottom until he can tell exactly how much unreported revenue has been illegally skimmed."

The Mormons were cocky, much more so than the day before, but Dalitz knew that their posturing was no more than another empty threat because if the fed had any evidence, he would have made an arrest instead of scarfing down a steak sandwich and two desserts. But what about the forensic accountant? Was there even such a thing? And if there was, could he really tear apart an operation from top to bottom the way White said he could? Until he knew for sure, Dalitz had no choice but to remain aggressive.

"Do yourself a favor, White, and take this cheap shakedown act of yours to one of the casinos down the street. Because like I told you yesterday, there is *nothing* I won't do to protect what belongs to me."

"I'm quite certain if Sid Klein were here, he could attest to that fact, but do not underestimate what *I* am capable of doing to gain possession of what the Lord has declared to be rightfully ours."

Blah, blah, blah. Same shit different day. Still, Dalitz wondered why White would make such a big show of trotting out the top local fed and the accountant unless he held a trump card that he was waiting until just the right moment to play. Another witness? Because if they had one, Dalitz knew it would be impossible to prevent the rat from testifying without knowing who the rat was. So, until he knew the score, would maintain the position that the best defense was a good offense.

"You're out of your league, White. No matter what move you think you're big enough to make, in the end I'll be scraping both you and that cockroach of yours off the bottom of my shoe."

"I advise you to be careful, Morris. Pride goeth before a fall."

"Take your best shot. My lawyers will keep the feds and anybody else you throw at me chasing their tails for years."

"I have all the time in the world but for you the clock is ticking. Do you want to do this the easy way and sell the Desert Inn to Brother Cliff, or would you prefer to squander the precious few years you have left waging a war you cannot win?"

Dalitz gazed around the casino at people throwing away good money after bad. Looked out the window at hotel guests playing tennis and enjoying themselves at the figure-eight shaped swimming pool, realizing that the Mormons were not some rival gang who recruited membership at night court and at the pool hall. They were an army that bred its soldiers with almighty purpose, putting God on everything like ketchup and growing fat with misguided morality. He caught a glimpse of Vernon White straightening his pocket square. A condescending prick. But a prick with an army.

"I've always gotten a kick out of taking down punks who think they're tough enough to steal what belongs to me, but while I was relaxing in Palm Springs the other day, I took stock in my life and realized that there would be limited pleasure in cutting off the balls of a cockroach like your car salesman. Partly because he's just a cog in the Mormon machine who can be replaced as many times as necessary, but mostly because I wasn't seeing the big picture." Dalitz thought about deep sea fishing on his yacht and how good his young wife looked sunning herself in a bikini at their villa in Acapulco. "I've accomplished more in my lifetime than most men could in a hundred and I can see now that maybe it's time to eliminate the stress, step back and enjoy every pleasure my money can buy."

"I'm pleased that you have arrived at the prudent decision to lay down your sword and surrender to the inevitable."

"Slow down, White. I don't have to sell this place in order to retire."

"You do unless you want to spend that retirement in prison."

The same empty threat, but Dalitz saw no percentage in squandering his remaining years fighting a protracted holy war, especially if the enemy's arsenal included a forensic accountant. He walked through the casino to the bar, predators behind him step for step. Told the bartender to pour two fingers of single malt from a special bottle he had brought back from Scotland a few years earlier. Looked at the glass for what seemed like minutes before picking it up and letting the golden-brown liquid roll down his throat.

"Okay White. Have your flunky draw up a sales agreement and I'll sign it next week."

"You'll sign it tomorrow, cockroach." Chandler could taste the victory. Felt the power. "I'll be here at 10:00 in the morning."

CHAPTER 11

"See that middle-aged guy with the long sideburns over by the dollar slots," Harry said to Big Paulie who had arrived at the Desert Inn half an hour earlier with a plane full of high rollers in tow. "Is he with your junket?"

"Never seen him before," said the robust New Yorker in a blue sport shirt and heavy gold chain hanging from his neck. "Who is he?"

"No clue, but for the past ten minutes he hasn't taken his eyes off Moe for even a second."

Big Paulie saw Dalitz talking to the shift supervisor in the blackjack pit, then looked past him to the cocktail lounge that rattled in high gear at a time of the morning when it was usually quiet. Where Howard Hughes was standing at the end of the busy bar pouring a shot of whiskey into his coffee.

"You sure the egg isn't staring at Hughes? Famous guy like him attracts a lot of attention."

"Could be, but I get the feeling something's not right about him."

"Probably nothing, Harry," Big Paulie told him as he traded

smiles with a keno cutie, then turned toward the casino cage where he was needed to okay credit for his first timers. "I'll catch up with you later."

Harry scoped out the reporters and cameramen congregating in the lounge, having been summoned for a press conference announcing that the Las Vegas Strip was about to change forever. Out from under the thumb of organized crime and steered toward a respectability that would legitimize the way casinos did business. And right on cue the man in the tan sports jacket and perma-pressed Wrangler slacks marched with a swagger into the casino, armed with a briefcase containing a cashiers check for $2 million and an agreement for the remaining $8 million to be paid to Dalitz upon regulatory approval by the Nevada Gaming Commission. Head held high as he was about to bask in heavenly light as champion of both church and community as the hotel that would soon bear his name set into motion the church's plan to create a monopoly by controlling the biggest properties on the Las Vegas Strip.

"Come on," Chandler said as he approached Dalitz. "Let's go up to the office and get this deal done."

"Don't you want to talk to the reporters?"

"After we sign the papers."

"Are you sure you want to wait? Looks like Howard Hughes is trying to hijack your press conference," said Dalitz as he gestured toward the lanky Texan who was holding court at the end of the bar.

"Quit stalling."

"Hold on a minute, Cliff. When one of the richest men in the country has something to say, we should see what he's up to."

And see they did, as Howard Hughes announced to the press that he was the new owner of the Desert Inn.

"Drinks are on me, fellas," Hughes called out as he swilled his spiked coffee. "I signed the papers an hour ago."

Mr. Hughes. How much did you pay for the hotel?

"$13 million."

Do you have plans to buy any other Strip hotels?

"I'm going to buy them all."

Does this mean that you're going to be living in Las Vegas?

"I'm here for good. Just moved upstairs into the penthouse."

Word on the street was that Cliff Chandler was going to buy the Desert Inn.

"Who's Cliff Chandler?"

"We have a deal!" Chandler screamed at Dalitz.

"I made a better deal with Hughes."

"I'll kill you, you fucking Jew gangster!" exploded the jilted car dealer as he swung his briefcase wildly at Dalitz's head and missed.

Flashbulbs popped. Film rolled. The press eating it up as the man who had built his reputation on righteousness and wholesome family values exposed his true colors.

While junketeers attacked the dice tables, everyone else in the casino crowded around the action as Dalitz waved off security so that photographers could keep shooting while the enraged Chandler continued to wildly swing the briefcase. Like watching a matador sidestepping an angry bull, tourists took snapshots they would show friends when asked if anything exciting happened on their Las Vegas vacation. Harry smiled. Big Paulie laughed his ass off. The middle-aged man with long sideburns watched closely but displayed no reaction. A grandmother with a do-it-yourself bouffant dye job got too close with her Instamatic camera and was conked in the head by the briefcase, prompting her husband put an end to the spectacle by knocking Chandler out with one punch.

Order was quickly restored as tourists went back to chasing jackpots while the three Rogers, career criminals all by coincidence named Roger that Dalitz kept on call for special jobs, slapped Chandler awake and yanked him to his feet.

"You'll pay for this, Dalitz! This is not over!" screamed Chandler as he was manhandled toward the door. "THIS IS NOT OVER!"

Dalitz gloated with the arrogance of uncontested power at how easily he had conned Vernon White with that load of baloney about retiring as Howard Hughes announced to the press that the current management structure of the Desert Inn would remain in place. Meaning that essentially nothing had changed as Dalitz would still call the shots from behind his massive horseshoe desk, having been paid $13 million for a license to steal from the casino he no longer owned. And that no matter how much political clout the Mormons had, or how loud Cliff Chandler or Vernon White or God himself squawked, not only would the Nevada Gaming Commission not block an expedited sale of the Desert Inn to a man the stature of Howard Hughes, no one would ever again have cause to send a forensic accountant anywhere near the place.

CHAPTER 12

"I still have the $10 million from the bank loan. We can use it to buy Caesars or the Sands," pressed Chandler, grasping at straws as he tried to rebound from rock bottom. Needing a shave. Sporting a black eye and the same clothes he'd had on twenty-four hours earlier. Reeking of failure and hiding out in his office behind a closed door, denying browsers in his showroom a glimpse of the man who, like a rookie car salesman, had made a big noise but was unable to close the deal.

"Pretty girl," said Vernon White as he picked up one of the framed family photos displayed on the credenza.

"My daughter, Annie."

"How old is she?"

"Seventeen." Then Chandler added proudly. "She's been accepted to start college at BYU in the fall."

"Plans can change."

"What are you trying to say?"

"That *we* are not going to buy Caesars, the Sands or anything else."

"I'm not excusing what I did, but that's not why we lost the D.I. deal. Howard Hughes had already signed the papers an hour before I got there."

"Mr. Hughes would have been a non-factor had your ego not cost us leverage by alerting Morris Dalitz to the fact that we had a witness prepared testify under oath about his skimming of unreported revenue." White used his handkerchief to erase a smudge from the glass, then put the framed photo back in its place. "So, listen very carefully when I say that if you have any future contact with Dalitz, Hughes or representatives of any other Strip hotel, your seventeen-year-old daughter's acceptance to Brigham Young University will be rescinded and she will spend the next two years on a church mission attempting to convert natives in the Belgian Congo."

"Don't threaten my daughter."

"I'm certain you can imagine the degree of undesired attention a pretty blond teenager would attract in darkest Africa."

"I'm not going to warn you again," said Chandler as he rose from his chair and aggressively faced Vernon White. "Do *not* threaten my daughter."

"I can assure you that Annie's college career will begin as scheduled, as long as it is understood that you are no longer part of the church's plan to enter the casino business."

"You can't cut me out. I've been the public face of that plan since the beginning."

"Be grateful for all the Lord has bestowed upon you," said Vernon White as he looked at a painting of the car dealer alongside his bulldog Cliff Jr. that hung on the wall behind the desk. "But do not forget for even one second that those blessings can just as easily be taken away."

"Are you telling me that the Lord refuses to forgive one mistake?" Chandler assessed the man he was bound by religious duty to honor, all-of-a-sudden unsure of White's intentions as things didn't seem to add up. "Or are you trying to cash in on that one mistake because you want *your* name on the sign in front of the Desert Inn?"

"The wise men in Salt Lake have always found it in their best interest to turn a blind eye to even my most extreme methods, as long as the desired result is achieved. So, for your sake, I suggest that from this moment forward you confine your business activity to selling automobiles or you will discover the hard way just how extreme those methods can be." He again looked at the photo of Cliff Chandler's pretty seventeen-year-old daughter. "Have I made myself clear?"

Vernon White did not wait for an answer.

Chandler slumped back into his chair, looking around an office filled with reminders of past acclaim never to be reprised because of a public humiliation brought about by a misguided belief that he could prevail mano a mano against a gangster who had no more decency than the devil himself. Who was the devil himself. Who had been correct in saying that he was a cog in a machine who could be replaced, because he had been replaced. His reputation shattered to the point where even God had turned a deaf ear. He closed his eyes and once again prayed for forgiveness. For guidance of how he could right such an all-encompassing wrong, only to have his pleas interrupted as the office door swung open before the amen.

"Get out!"

"Most men are excited when I walk into a room," said Sunny as she shut the door, then sat down across the desk and made herself comfortable.

"Men of low character, I can assure you," said Chandler as he sized up the eye-catching brunette in a pink mini-skirt and low-cut blouse. "Now get out of here. I have work to do."

"By work, I assume you mean hiding like a scared little boy until the mess you've gotten yourself into blows over. But it won't go away by itself, and I don't see anybody else here offering support." Sunny reached over and plucked the morning *Review-Journal* out of the waste basket and spread it out on Chandler's desk. A front-page photo of the enraged car dealer attacking Moe Dalitz staring up at them. "If you expect to ever find a way to make that embarrassment go away, you're going to need my help."

"Help from a street walker?"

"Call girl." Then she added proudly, "A $500 a night call girl."

"I'm certainly not paying $500 for whatever advice you think might help me."

"Not advice, Cliff. Information. And the price is $20,000."

"I told you before to get out."

"I'm sure if you think about it for a moment, you'll realize that's a very small price to pay for information you can use to restore your reputation." Sunny crossed her tanned legs, slowly to hold his attention. "*And* get control of the Desert Inn."

Chandler ripped the newspaper to shreds and threw it back into the trash.

"You know darn well that Howard Hughes bought the Desert Inn."

"Are you sure about that?"

"What are you getting at?"

"The answer to that question will cost you $20,000."

"Why would I give that kind of money to a whore?"

"When God delivers a miracle, do you think it's wise to insult the messenger?"

"What could a person like you possibly know about God?"

"I was raised in a spiritual family."

"Not of the Mormon faith, I can assure you."

"My parents are what some people call Golden Rulers. They taught my sisters and I the difference between right and wrong, and that we should treat others the way we would like them to treat us."

"That's not spirituality," Chandler scoffed. "That's not anything."

"It's the only belief system any person should ever need. Core values that allowed me to become a good person, even though you still think of me as nothing but a whore."

"You are a whore."

"I'm a call girl who treats people with respect, which is a lot more than I can say for you."

Chandler knew that the man upstairs worked in mysterious ways, but was it possible that God had responded to his prayers with a lifeline delivered on the wings of a fallen woman? The answer to that question could not to be found in the *Book of Mormon*. Guidance could not be sought at the temple and certainly not from the special emissary of the

Quorum of the Twelve Apostles who only minutes before had in no uncertain terms threatened him to back off.

"Do you want to spend the rest of your life selling Chevys to people who snicker behind your back," she asked him. "Or do you want a chance at redemption?"

A successful car salesman could read people. Could tell the lookers from the buyers. The deceitful from the honorable. But as he looked into Sunny's eyes was confused by what he saw. Looked again. Same thing. This woman was sincere, but what could she possibly know that he and Vernon White did not? And even if she did know something that would put the situation in a different light, there was no way that he was going to hand over twenty grand to a woman he had known for only a few minutes. A woman who made her living screwing men for money. A woman he would not, under any circumstance, allow to screw him.

"If you're as good a person as you say you are, why demand money? Why don't you just tell me what it is you know?"

"For the same reason you don't give cars away."

"It's not the same thing."

"It's exactly the same thing."

"$20,000 is a lot of money."

"I'm offering a chance to reclaim your reputation and gain control of the Desert Inn, and you want to haggle about the price?"

"Only a fool would hand over that kind of money without knowing exactly what he's buying."

"Sorry I wasted your time, Cliff. I'm sure it won't be too difficult to find another buyer for the information I have. Moe

Dalitz maybe, or that well-dressed man I just saw leave your office."

Chandler stiffened. His eyes narrowed.

"I came to you first because I assumed you would be the most motivated, but I guess you don't care what the town thinks of you." Sunny stood, straightened her skirt then turned toward the door. "Good luck with the rest of your life."

"Wait."

It was at that moment Cliff Chandler realized that the Lord was challenging him to atone for his meltdown and prove his value to the church. He believed it. He had to believe it because it was the only straw left to grasp. A challenge to step up and grab a chance for redemption by following the unorthodox path being set before him. A path certain to be strewn with obstacles. The first being that a call girl would never deliver the goods without getting the money up front and he refused to pay one red cent until he heard what Sunny had to say. A standoff until she pointed to the ripped-up newspaper in the waste basket.

"Do you really want that photograph to be the defining moment of your life?"

He thought of derisive laughter in every living room in town whenever one of his commercials would come on television and knew that a longshot gamble on the word of a morally bankrupt woman was his only chance to earn back his reputation. Cliff Chandler had lived in Las Vegas all his life, and the first bet he ever made turned out to be in the form of a $20,000 check made payable to cash.

"You have my money. Now tell me what you came here to say."

"An awful lot of people in the showroom saw a call girl walk into your office," Sunny said as she folded the check and put it in her purse. "So, don't try to pull a fast one by stopping payment or I'll scream so loud at the bank that you'll be on the front page for a month."

"You have my word. Now talk."

"I know better than anyone that all men are not created equal."

"Stop speaking in riddles."

"Howard Hughes has a Texas-sized cock."

"What the heck does that have to do with anything?"

"The man in the penthouse at the Desert Inn does not."

CHAPTER 13

"Let's say for the sake of argument that the man in the penthouse *is* a phony. Where's the real Howard Hughes?"

"Dalitz had him killed."

Police Lieutenant R.P. Sampson watered a potted geranium that provided a solitary splash of color to his fluorescently lit office, then closed the door to keep the conversation with Cliff Chandler private.

"Did the prostitute tell you that too?"

"It makes perfect sense."

"No, it doesn't," the twenty-six-year veteran in the sharply pressed tan uniform told his closest friend. "It defies all logic that Moe Dalitz would murder one of the richest and most recognizable men in America and replace him with a looka-like. Howard Hughes knows presidents and dates movie stars, so who do you think an imposter would fool?"

"He fooled everyone at the press conference. And if Dalitz keeps him out of sight in that penthouse, no one will ever know the truth. That's why you have to help me expose the fraud."

"Get it through your thick head that the Desert Inn deal is dead and concentrate on selling cars," advised the policeman as he opened a window to keep from gagging on the rancid parlay of body odor and yesterday's cologne. "Which is sound advice considering I heard through the grapevine that Vernon White ordered you to stand down."

"An order I must respectfully disobey."

"What the heck is wrong with you, Cliff? Vernon White represents Temple Square, which means that while he's here he has authority over every Mormon stake president, bishop, elder and car dealer in Las Vegas."

"You don't know him like I do, R.P." Chandler grimaced as he caught a whiff of himself. "White crosses the line between right and wrong to suit his own needs, and I'm not going to stand down until I know for sure that he is indeed acting in the interest of the church and not the interest of himself."

"You had better not let anybody else hear you talk like that, or you might find yourself excommunicated. Not to mention that any more headlines like today and you'll be out of the car business. And what about Sheryl and the kids? Haven't you humiliated them enough?"

"My family will understand."

"Why? Because you insist that they respect your judgement while you ignore everybody else's? You've been a know-it-all ever since that summer at my uncle's ranch when we were kids and you were warned not to tease the mule. But you did anyway, and that ornery cuss kicked your backside clear out of the barn."

"We're not kids anymore."

"Then stop acting like one and put a stop to this nonsense, or this time I guarantee you're going to get kicked a lot harder."

"You're my best friend, R.P." Chandler knew the path to redemption would be fraught with challenges, but did not expect to be confronted with an obstacle so close to home. "I don't understand why you won't help me."

"Because you're not being rational." He looked at Chandler's shiner that had turned a hideous shade of bluish yellow. "You need to put a raw steak on that eye. And you need to let this whole Hughes business go."

"What I need is for you to go to the Desert Inn and take that imposter's fingerprints."

"Without probable cause, law enforcement has no legal right to enter Howard Hughes's residence, even if that residence is a hotel room. And even if I could, you know darn well that's out of my jurisdiction because until they merge the two departments like they keep saying they're going to do, any action by a Las Vegas Police Department officer on the Strip needs to be carried out in conjunction with the county sheriff's department. And because the sheriff is in Moe Dalitz's pocket, even with probable cause there is no way I could get anywhere near Howard Hughes at the Desert Inn."

"But it's *not* Hughes. It's an imposter."

"We don't know that."

"Yes, we do."

"Because some prostitute told you he doesn't measure up?"

"I know what it must sound like, R.P., but the Lord spoke to me through that woman. And it doesn't matter that the Desert Inn is out of your jurisdiction. All you have to do is flash your badge, get the fingerprints and you'll be out of there before anybody knows what happened."

"I would never go against procedure for any reason, even if Vernon White himself asked me. So, show me the consideration of respecting the oath I swore as a police officer."

"You can be a real jerk sometimes."

"The rules are black and white."

"So, you would throw me in jail if I snuck into the movies like we did when we were kids?"

"No gray area and no free passes for friends, so do yourself a favor and accept the fact that you lost and move on."

"I've never lost at anything in my life."

"Of course, you have, Cliff. It's just that your ego won't allow you to admit it. Like the time you wouldn't speak to me for a week after I beat you at Scrabble."

"Quay is not a word."

"Go home and clean yourself up, Cliff. Get a good night sleep and, God willing, you'll see things differently in the morning."

"If you won't help me, I'll figure out a way to get the fingerprints on my own."

"Even if you could, without official police involvement you would have no proof that they came from the man in the penthouse. No admissible proof of anything. The prints would be worthless."

"In court maybe. But you could check them and find out who the imposter is, then review his criminal history for something that connects him to Dalitz."

CHAPTER 14

It was just a simple cheeseburger on a toasted sesame seed bun but, for Harry's money, not even the chef at the Sky Room who Moe Dalitz imported from the Ritz in Paris could make it as well as Lew at the luncheonette. And after savoring the final bite and crunching the last few potato chips on his plate, Harry spun around on his stool and looked at the eye-filling blonde he had been checking out in the mirror for the past twenty minutes. Fresh face and girl next door pretty. Sexy without trying in a white sweater and bell bottom jeans. Long legs stretched out in a booth with her back against the window, picking at a plate of tuna salad as she turned pages of *Kiss Me Deadly* by Mickey Spillane.

"Have you gotten to the part where the bad guys try to blow him up?" Harry asked as he walked over to the booth.

"Not yet," she said without looking up from her book. "I'm only to the part where some jerk bothers me while I'm eating my lunch."

"May I join you?" Harry asked, not waiting for an answer as he sat down across from her, captivated by blue eyes with specs of silver and long straight hair so blond it was almost snow-white.

"Please leave me alone."

"I'm Harry Lake."

"You say that like it's spelled with capital letters."

"I apologize for intruding, but Mickey Spillane is one of my favorite authors."

"Does that line ever work?" she asked, finally taking a good look at the man in the stylishly tailored cream-colored suit as she closed her book and sat up straight in the booth. "I suppose if I had been reading Dr. Seuss you would have said the same thing."

"Did you know that before Dr. Seuss started writing for children, his books were quite risqué?"

"That couldn't possibly be true."

"Go to the library and check out *The Seven Lady Godivas,*" he said, lifting his gaze from her tight-fitting sweater. "Or better yet, let's go together."

"Don't you have to get back to work, Mr. Lake?"

"Sorry if I've offended you by coming on so strong. Will you allow me to start over?" He pushed aside a bottle of Orange Crush spouting an elbow straw, then reached across the table and with mock formality shook her hand. "My name is Harry Lake, and I hope you will allow me to get to know you better."

"Charlotte," she said, her defenses beginning to crack. "Charlotte Kaye. And I still think you're awfully forward."

"Things move fast in Vegas. But I suppose you wouldn't know that being new in town."

"What makes you assume that I'm new in town?"

"I've never seen you before."

"And you know every girl in Las Vegas?"

"I would have remembered seeing you."

Charlotte rolled her eyes.

"You're from Iowa or Indiana. Some small town in the Midwest."

"Is it that obvious?"

"It's refreshing."

"Baloney."

"Can't you take a compliment?"

"How come in a city with so many glamorous women, you try to pick up a girl at a luncheonette. Are you a pimp?"

Harry laughed.

"Then why me?"

"Because there's a certain freshness that sets you apart from those other women. A beauty that doesn't require makeup and flash."

"That's another line, Harry."

"I meant every word of it."

"Baloney."

"Don't they say *bullshit* where you come from?"

"Good girls don't. And if you're not a pimp, I apologize."

"Will you have dinner with me tonight?"

The busboy made a racket clearing dishes from the next booth, so he asked again to make sure she had heard him.

"Take your foot off the gas, Harry."

"Exactly where in Iowa are you from?"

"Wisconsin. Elkhorn. It's a nice town and I enjoyed growing

up there, but on my last birthday I turned twenty-three, and once a girl reaches that milestone in a speck on the map like Elkhorn her only options are becoming a waitress or marrying the boy next door and having his kids." Charlotte took a bite of tuna salad, then bent the straw and washed it down with a long sip of Orange Crush. "My parents were killed in a car accident a few years ago and I don't have any other family, so when my friend Barb's boyfriend dumped her and she decided to chase the bright lights of Hollywood, I packed my entire life into two suitcases and got on the Greyhound with her."

"This isn't Hollywood."

"But the lights are brighter. Something so intoxicating about all the neon that we got off the bus and checked into a small kitchenette at the Bali Hai motel. We had a lot of fun for about a week, then Barb's boyfriend showed up and took her back to Elkhorn. I liked it here, so I decided to stay and look for a job."

"I'll give you a job."

"You said you weren't a pimp."

"If you're still at the Bali Hai that makes us neighbors. I live at the Desert Inn."

"You *live* at the Desert Inn? Isn't that awfully expensive?"

"I'm president of the hotel." Harry handed her his business card. "What kind of job would you like? Hostess in the Sky Room? Lifeguard? Pro shop at the golf course? If you can dance, I'll put you in the *Hello America* revue in the Crystal Room, and if you can't dance, I'll put you in the show anyway. Whatever you want."

"Going out to dinner would make working for you awkward."

"Then I'll get you a job at another hotel. Or at Sears or

Woolworth's or the public library where you can read Mickey Spillane all day."

"You have that kind of influence?"

"It's called juice, and Vegas runs on it."

CHAPTER 15

"Don't you know when to quit?" snapped Harry, angry that Cliff Chandler had blindsided him as he flipped through jazz LPs at Garwood Van's Musicland kitty-corner from the Sahara Hotel.

"I have a proposition for you."

"Like last week at Churchill Downs when you threatened me with prison if I didn't turn rat?"

Harry continued thumbing through the M's, where he always looked first because it was the section that contained many of his favorites. Miles, Monk, Mulligan and Shelly Manne. He preferred jazz to the Top 40 pushing through the store speakers, as the complex rhythms took him somewhere, right now wishing that destination was far away from Cliff Chandler.

"At least listen to what I have to say."

"Moe sold the Desert Inn out from under you, so what could you possibly have to say?"

"Come on, Harry. Let's bury the hatchet," said Chandler as he gestured to the briefcase he was carrying.

"You going to hit me with it?"

"It's a peace offering."

"Peace is for hippies. Get lost."

"Aren't you even curious as to what's inside?"

"Okay, I'll bite," Harry said, knowing that Chandler would not stop bugging him until he heard him out. "What's in the briefcase?"

Chandler looked around to make sure no other customers were close by, then popped the latches to reveal banded stacks of $1,000 bills.

"$500,000, Harry. And it's all yours."

"No thanks."

"That's half a million dollars!"

Harry continued to flip through the M's. Mingus, Maybern, Hugh Masekela.

"Nobody can afford to turn down that kind of money. Think about what it could buy."

"Enough money buys the freedom to live life on your own terms. Freedom to do whatever you want whenever you want without ever having to answer to anyone. And, for me, what's inside that briefcase of yours isn't even a drop in the bucket."

"Hey, Harry," called the teenage girl with a sandy blond ponytail working at the counter. "That Ronnie Scott LP you ordered just came in."

"Thanks, Suzy. Keep it by the register for me, will you please." Then Harry turned back to Chandler. "And don't make like the money is a gift. What's your pitch?"

"You and I both know that the man in the penthouse at the Desert Inn is not Howard Hughes. All you have to do is help me prove he's an imposter and the cash is yours."

"Don't think that you can get your hands on the D.I. by exposing a fraud, because there's a fatal flaw in that plan."

"Which is?"

"I'm in a good mood today, so the answer to that question will only cost you a grand."

Harry plucked a $1,000 bill from one of the banded stacks inside the briefcase, then motioned for the girl at the counter to come over and handed it to her. "Ring up that Ronnie Scott LP and keep the change."

"That's a $1,000 bill."

"Buy yourself something nice."

"Thank you, Harry! Thank you!"

"Better yet," he added, taking two more bills from the briefcase and handing them to her. "When you get off work, walk down the street to Gaudin Ford and buy yourself that new Mustang convertible they have displayed out front."

Harry smiled as he watched the ecstatic teenager float back to her post.

"You're awfully generous with my money," groused Chandler. "And sending her to the competition no less."

"A small price to keep from making a fool of yourself again like you did the other day."

"Okay, I paid. What's the fatal flaw in my plan?"

"The man in the penthouse *is* Howard Hughes."

CHAPTER 16

"Three hundred bucks says that the next guy who walks past here will be wearing red alligator shoes," said Harry as he handed a suitcase to the bell captain.

"It's a bet."

"And keep the bag close because Big Paulie will come by for it in a few minutes."

"Won't let it out of my sight," said Freddy as he placed it behind the bell desk rather than stowing it with the other checked luggage, then busted out a smile as a man walked past wearing Bermuda shorts and pool sandals.

Harry paid off the bet that was not really a bet as suggesting propositions with zero chance of winning was his way of compensating Freddy for keeping his eyes open, as the smartly uniformed bell captain had the lowdown on everything that happened at the Desert Inn and most of what happened around town.

"What's the dope on that guy over there?" asked Harry as he pointed toward the middle-aged man with long sideburns who was staring at Dalitz drinking coffee in the cocktail lounge.

"Never seen him before."

"Come on, Freddy," he said, raising his voice to be heard over the commotion of a hot craps table where junketeers took a final shot at winning back some of their money before the charter flight home. "You can make every face that's ever walked into this casino. Look again."

"Sorry, Harry. I can't place him."

"This isn't the first time he's been scoping out Moe, so keep your eye on him for anything suspicious and let me know if he comes around again."

"Will do, Harry," agreed Freddy as he absorbed a flirtatious smile from the raven-haired cocktail waitress with tits like torpedoes he had been undecided about a few days earlier.

"Looks like you took her to see Bobby Darin."

"The broad screwed me so hard I thought my pecker was going to fall off."

"That smile says she's up for an encore."

"But she wants me to take her to an expensive dinner first. I tell you, Harry, every broad in this town is on the make for something."

"You just haven't found the right girl yet," said Harry, then started to walk away.

"Wait a minute." Freddy motioned for him to come back. "I don't know if it means anything, but Stiffy Woo at the Plush Horse has a brother-in-law who got pinched for passing bad paper, and when he went downtown the other day to bail him out, he saw that putz Chandler getting really chummy with a cop lieutenant named Sampson, then go in his office and close the door."

Harry chewed on that bit of information as he walked away to join his boss in the lounge, brushing past Big Paulie without saying a word. Watching closely as Freddy handed the suitcase to the man who was on his way back to New York where, just as after every junket, he would deliver it to a Wall Street banker. But today, instead of cash from the skim that the banker would massage cleanly into a brokerage account belonging to Moe Dalitz, the suitcase was filled with dirty laundry. A test run to make sure that Sid Klein had disappeared before spilling everything he knew.

"Have a drink and relax," said Dalitz, noticing the unsettled look on Harry's face as they watched Big Paulie walk out the door. "Even if they do roust Paulie, all the feds can charge him with is transporting soiled Jockey shorts across state lines."

"Chandler cornered me again."

"What the fuck for? It's over and he lost."

"He doesn't think so."

"What did he threaten you with this time?"

"Money. Half a million to help him prove that Hughes is a phony."

"Did you tell him that the man upstairs *is* Howard Hughes?"

"Of course, I did."

"Then if he was stupid enough to offer the money you should have taken it."

"I don't ever want to give even the slightest impression that I'm not a hundred percent loyal to you." Harry lit a cigarette, then continued through a stream of smoke. "It's time to make good on your promise to cut me in for a piece of this place."

"Your slice of the skim not enough?"

"Crumbs, Moe. You promised me points in the hotel and my name on the license."

"As soon as the Hughes deal is approved by the Gaming Commission, my name won't even be on the license."

"But you can arrange it so mine is, right beside the name Howard Hughes. Make that happen, Moe. You know I've earned it."

"You're only thirty-one-years old. What's the rush?"

"How many times do I have to prove myself? I'm trusted with the keys to the kingdom whenever you go out of town, and I make myself vulnerable by providing you a buffer from law enforcement." Harry knew that allowing himself to become vulnerable was a risk worth taking if the reward was great enough, but not a risk worth taking if Dalitz was going to keep him spinning his wheels. "So, quit stalling, Moe. You know I've more than earned my piece of the action."

"Be patient, Harry. Your time will come."

"When, Moe?"

"When I tell you. Now if there's nothing else, I've got a date to shtup Angie Dickinson."

It was a line Dalitz often used to extricate himself from an unwanted conversation, but Harry wouldn't let him off the hook.

"We need to take Chandler seriously, Moe. I just got word that before he approached me with the cash, he spent time downtown with some police lieutenant."

"City cops have no jurisdiction on the Strip without an okay from the sheriff, and I own the sheriff. So, who gives a shit?"

"We should, because I guarantee that Chandler is not going

to let this go. And any man who refuses to accept the fact that he lost is dangerous because you can't handicap what he might do next."

"Forget him, Harry. He's a clown," Dalitz stated with confidence as he shot the cuffs of his white-on-white shirt and adjusted his diamond cufflinks.

"He may have lost respectability by making a public spectacle of himself, but he still has friends in this town with a lot of clout. Friends who are not particularly fond of the way we do business." Harry was irritated that there was no ashtray on the table. Irritated that Dalitz was dragging his feet instead of coming across with his piece of the action. Irritated that the renewed threat of Cliff Chandler was not being taken seriously. "I saw it in his eyes, Moe. He is *not* going to go away quietly, and we can't afford to take any chances."

"You worry too much, Harry," said Dalitz as he motioned for the cocktail waitress to bring an ashtray, then waited until she was out of earshot before continuing. "But if it will make you sleep any better, let's get rid of that cockroach once and for all."

"You can't kill everybody who gets in your way. Besides, whether you are in town or not, it would be so obvious you were behind Chandler's murder that all those friends with clout would scream so loud even the sheriff couldn't save you."

"Then we'll bring in a hitter from back east."

"You're missing the point, Moe. No matter who pulls the trigger it would still blow back on you. Besides, violence is never the answer. There's always a better way. A smarter way."

"Sometimes violence is the only way."

"Stop thinking like a gangster."

"What kind of farkakte world is this where we can't ignore Chandler, and we can't kill him?" grumbled Dalitz as he pushed away his coffee. "How about we kill his dog?"

"That would probably bring more heat than killing Chandler, because everybody in town loves that dog."

"Then let's have some more fun with that cockroach. Tonight, after his dealership closes, send a couple of the Rogers over there to put sand in all the gas tanks."

CHAPTER 17

"What do you say? What do you know?"

"Never get in the ring with Sonny Liston or plead guilty to anything except being hungry," Harry cracked to the fat-faced bartender at the Green Shack as he and Charlotte found two stools and made themselves comfortable. "And we *are* hungry."

"Hey, Margie," the bartender called to a passing waitress. "Bring a couple pan fried specials for my friends."

"This place serves the best southern fried chicken in Vegas," Harry told Charlotte, then it occurred to him that he may have jumped the gun. "You do like fried chicken, right?"

"As long as I can eat it without having to worry about using the wrong fork."

"You didn't like the Sky Room?"

"Last night was wonderful, Harry," she quickly backpedaled. "Champagne, candlelight and amazing food. It's just that I was intimidated because I had never been to a place that fancy."

"I was trying to impress you and I guess I overdid it, but tonight you're going to see the flipside of Harry Lake. That's why I suggested you dress casually," he said, liking the way she looked in a jean jacket over a flowery peasant dress. Himself wearing a blue V-neck sweater and dark corduroy flares as he called for the bartender to bring them a couple beers.

The place was hopping, and Charlotte was fascinated by her first look at life away from the Strip. No glitz or flash, just regular people enjoying regular meals as they would in any other town. She and Harry talked about music. She liked the Monkees while he dug Thelonious Monk. Current movies. She liked romantic comedies while he had seen tough guy Lee Marvin in *Point Blank* three times. She watched *Bewitched* and *Get Smart* while Harry could not remember the last time he had turned on his television. But opposites attracted. Charlotte was relaxed and having a good time, losing herself in eyes the color of milk chocolate when the beer caused her to accidentally burp. She was mortified. But Harry cut the tension by working up a belch of his own.

"Even?"

"Even," she smiled, then leaned over and kissed him gently on the lips.

Never in her life had Charlotte made the first move, having been raised in a puritanical household by parents blind to the fact that the world was now populated by a younger generation that not only questioned authority but made its own rules. She was not supposed to fall for the smooth-talking playboy, a plan that went quickly sideways upon discovering Harry to be down to earth, funny and every bit a gentleman. But she feared she had blown it the night before by not inviting him inside after he had treated her to an elegant dinner, taken her to the Folies Bergere and held her hand while escorting her home. In the morning, however, her phone rang with a second chance that she was determined not to screw up.

The fried chicken was as good as advertised, but Charlotte played it safe by not having another beer until they got to the Top Hat Ballroom, a run-down slot joint, a stone's throw from the downtown casinos of Glitter Gulch. A place Harry popped into once in a while to play pinball, a game he used to hustle as a kid in New York. A game Charlotte confessed that she had never played, causing him to wonder about what must have been a total lack of culture in Elkhorn, Wisconsin.

The Top Hat was a place where people on the downside of advantage told stories of what used to be and what might have been. And amid the lingering essence of failure and odiferous funk, Charlotte wondered why Harry would bring her to a place like that as it could not possibly be the flipside of a man who enjoyed champagne and caviar. Was it payback for complaining about the Sky Room or just a power trip to see how far he could push her? But when the change girl, battle scarred old hen actually, waved hello and called him by name, Charlotte knew that she actually was seeing the real Harry Lake.

The more she got to know him the better she liked him, but feared what would happen should she allow him to get close enough to know the real Charlotte Kaye. Became fascinated as she watched a bum stuffing nickels into a slot machine, and asked Harry why a man like that would gamble away what little money he had instead of spending it on food or shoes without holes in them.

"I once saw a guy at the Dunes lose a million at the craps table, and instead of spending his last five bucks on breakfast he bet it on a hard eight."

"Why would he do that?"

"Because Vegas is the one place on earth where no matter how bad things are, you can get flush with just one pull of a handle or one hot roll with the dice. And if a gambler quits with even a dollar left in his pocket, he'll go out of his mind wondering if one more bet would have changed his luck."

"But this poor man probably won't eat tonight," said Charlotte, feeling guilty about the fried chicken and biscuits they had just enjoyed as she saw the one-armed bandit snatch the bum's last nickel. "Should I give him some money?"

Harry waved over the change girl and traded $2 for a roll of nickels. Then handed it to Charlotte.

"Give him this instead. Because what he wants more than anything else is a chance."

Charlotte walked cautiously toward the man with matted hair and dirty hands whose jacket and pants looked as if they had come from the bottom of a trash can. And when she gave him that chance, his eyes lit brighter than if she would have staked him to three square meals for a month.

"How did you get to be so smart?" Charlotte asked as she pulled Harry close and kissed him, a jolt of excitement shooting through her as he kissed her back.

"Vegas has a way of wising people up."

"Tell me more, Harry. About you I mean."

"Too much too soon and you might lose interest."

"I've got all night."

It seemed like it took almost all night for Harry to let her win at pinball, and when she finally did a hand reached up and put a dime on the machine.

"I'm next. How much you wanna play for, chickie?"

First a bum and now a midget with a mustache the size of a cat made Charlotte feel as if she had fallen down a rabbit hole.

"This gentleman of obvious refinement is Hollywood," Harry told her. "Make sure you hold onto your purse with both hands."

"Why you gotta be like that, Harry?" complained the midget as he pulled a case of empty beer bottles over to the pinball machine, stood on it and deposited the dime. "I got more class than to dip into your broad's bag."

"Whose bag?"

"Your tomato here."

"Who?"

"Your tamale, your chippie, your gash." The midget couldn't figure out why Harry didn't get the picture. "Don't you understand English? I'm talking' about this broad who's standin' right here."

"It's okay, Harry. I think he's cute."

"You got good taste, chickie. You should see some of my movies."

"Which are currently being screened in back rooms and at stag parties," clarified Harry.

"Doesn't mean I'm not a movie star. I got it where it counts." He winked at Charlotte. "If you know what I mean. I got so many broads beggin' for it, they have to take numbers like at the bakery."

Hollywood pulled back the plunger and powered the steel ball into play, manipulated the bumpers to the point where he almost rang up too many points, but eventually managed to lose the game.

"Once more," he said as he slammed a black casino chip on the glass. "Play you for $100 to make it interesting."

"I'm not going to let you hustle my girl, so go find a sucker somewhere else." Harry looked at the $100 casino chip. "Or did you already?"

"The biggest. Your pal Howard Hughes."

"Where is he?"

"You know Howard Hughes?" Charlotte asked Harry excitedly. "What's he like? Can I meet him?"

"Dammit, Hollywood. Where is he?"

"He was boozing it up over at the Mint, then all of a sudden threw a cuntload of chips up in the air like confetti on New Years Eve."

"How many chips?" Charlotte asked.

"Don't they teach you young broads anything at school? It's more than a shitload but not as much as a fuckload. Anyway, the one good thing about being small is that I scooped up a pocketful of those black beauties before anybody else hit the floor."

"Is he still there?" Harry demanded.

"Who?

"Hughes! Is he still at the Mint?"

"He picked up a couple hookers, then stole a cab on Fremont Street and tore the fuck out of there."

CHAPTER 18

Swilling tequila from the bottle, Howard Hughes cornholed a blonde whose face was buried between the legs of a petite brunette, then roughly shoved her aside ready to stick it to the dark-haired hooker who was naked except for a pair of dark stockings.

"Take 'em off."

"No."

"Do what I fucking tell you."

"No."

Hughes bounced off the bed then stepped to the other side of the motel room and took a roll of bills from his pants pocket. Threw $100 at her.

"Take 'em off."

"No!"

He hit her with another $100, but she held firm. $200 more finally persuading her to roll the stocking off one leg, then she hesitated before removing the other stocking to reveal a prosthetic leg.

"Take it off."

"My leg? Are you out of your mind?"

He threw $500 at her.

"I said take it off."

"I'm getting out of here, you fucking pervert."

She started to get up, but Hughes pushed her back on the bed and threw $1,000 at her. Finally, the price was right, and she removed the artificial leg, then screamed in pain as Hughes tried to force it into her pussy.

"STOP! YOU'RE HURTING ME!" She grabbed for the leg. "GIVE IT BACK!"

"You want it?" Hughes laughed as he got off the bed holding the leg above his head. "Come and get it."

She hopped awkwardly after him, Hughes taunting her like a schoolyard bully playing keep away.

"Give it back to her, you asshole," yelled the blonde as she grabbed for the leg.

Hughes pushed her away and when she came roaring back cracked her in the head with it. The brunette hopped after him as he climbed into his clothes then teased her by holding out the leg, but not close enough where she could grab it. Again, he tormented her. And again, laughing as he opened the door. She got close enough to lunge for it, but he stepped aside, leaving her to crash ass over elbows onto the asphalt parking lot. Other motel guests opened doors to catch a look at the naked one-legged hooker curled into a ball and crying as Hughes threw more money at her.

"Go buy some crutches, Hopalong," he laughed, waving the leg like a trophy as he got into the stolen taxi.

The motel manager raced out of the office threatening to call the police.

"You're not calling anybody," Hughes yelled as he tossed a handful of bills in his direction.

"Then get her out of here."

"She's yours now."

"What am I supposed to do with her?

"Anything you want. It's not like she can run away."

The taxi burned rubber out of the parking lot toward the lights of the Strip.

CHAPTER 19

"Which one of you assholes let him get out of here?" Dalitz screamed at the three Rogers as morning sun beamed through the windows of the Desert Inn penthouse.

Career criminals not afraid of anything or anyone except the man they answered to, the Rogers stood mute. But it took Dalitz only a moment to zero in on the one with sweat beading on his brow.

"I couldn't help it, Mr. Dalitz. I was sitting on the toilet when Hughes ran out. I thought we could get him back before anybody realized he was gone."

"Get the fuck out of here and find him! All of you!" Then Dalitz turned toward the sheriff, cowboy hat tilted over his eyes as he kicked back on the sofa. "And what about you? You just going to lounge around with your feet on my coffee table?"

"I've been up all night."

"Doing what? How the fuck can a man as famous as Howard Hughes go on a public bender without you and your Keystone Kops being able to find him?"

"We found the cab he stole parked out front of Pussycat A Go-Go."

"That's right next door!" Dalitz screamed as he looked out the window. "He was right under your fucking nose, and you let him get away?"

"Waitress told us he was only there for one drink, then took off. Nobody knew where."

"I don't want fucking excuses. For what I'm paying you, you should have had Hughes back here hours ago."

"Maybe if you paid me more, I would have."

Dalitz knocked the cowboy hat off the sheriff's head, then shot a look that burned right through him.

"Don't get tough with me, Moe. I'm the law in this county."

"Before I put you on the payroll you were nothing but a hick with a Cracker Jack badge shaking down hookers for hand jobs."

"I have to kick down part of the money you pay me to my top deputy who's in on everything, and that doesn't leave near enough left over for me to justify all the dirty jobs I do for you and all the secrets I have to keep."

"We'll talk about that later. Right now, get your lazy ass off my couch and find out where the fuck Hughes went!"

"The Tod Motel," said Harry, entering the penthouse as the sheriff picked up his hat and beat it out the door. "Turns out one of those hookers he took for a joyride had an artificial leg. After he roughed her up, Hughes stole it then showed up at Honest John's where he used the leg as a baseball bat to bust up the place, then dumped the cab next door at the Pussycat. I put the word out that we're offering a $50,000 reward for whoever spots him and right now every bartender, cabbie and working girl on the street is tearing the town apart looking for him."

"We have to find him fast, Harry. Because if we don't, somebody's going to call the cops on him. The real cops."

Harry had been racing full speed since dropping Charlotte off at the Bali Hai twelve hours earlier, on Hughes's trail from one shadowy corner to the next. Buying the silence of the desk clerk at the Tod and the bartender at Honest John's who said Hughes was flying so high on bennies he probably wouldn't sleep for days, making Harry certain he was still on the move. But he was always a half-step behind. *He just left, Harry* was a familiar response as was *You just missed him, Mr. Lake.* But Harry knew that Hughes would surface. $50,000 guaranteed it. But the clock was ticking as Harry knew exactly what was at stake if they didn't find the hopped-up millionaire double quick. Urgency in his pace as he got off the elevator, making a beeline through the casino toward a man he knew could help.

"Fifty dimes is a lot of money, Harry. Is that reward on the square?"

"Find him, Freddy, and it's all yours. But find him fast."

CHAPTER 20

"Excuse me, Mr. Sinatra. I'm sorry to interrupt your dinner."

"Then why did you?" said Frank Sinatra as he gave a quick once-over to the middle-aged man with long sideburns who was encroaching on his privacy in the Sky Room at the Desert Inn.

"I was hoping you'd do me a favor."

"You crash my party and now you want a favor?" Sinatra then looked to the powerfully built man seated at the end of the table. "Can you believe the balls on this guy, Jack? Teach him some manners."

"Glad to, Frank," said former heavyweight boxing champion Jack Dempsey as he stood and smashed a fist into his palm.

The glass-sided gourmet room grew silent as diners dressed to the nines watched the terrified man sweat bullets, then Sinatra busted out laughing.

"Relax, pally. Just our little joke. What's your name?"

"Ben Zorren."

"What can I do for you, Ben? You want an autograph?"

"Nothing like that, Mr. Sinatra," Zorren said, relieved that he still had his teeth. "You see that stacked blonde in the blue dress coming out of the ladies room? I'm trying to impress her, and it would help a lot if on your way out you could stop by our table and say hello."

"So you can show the broad what a big shot you are by telling me to get lost?" Sinatra was angry. "It's a tired bit, Zorren."

"That's not ..."

"Maybe I will stop by your table and tell her you have the clap."

"I'm sorry I bothered you, Mr. Sinatra. Please accept my apology for interrupting your dinner."

Zorren pulled out her chair as the stunning woman in the low-cut blue dress returned to their table. Her name was Gladys, a dancer in Lido de Paris at the Stardust, who on most nights after the show could be found on the arm of a big spender willing to blow his bankroll trying to get her legs in the air. They ate caviar and drank martinis under stars made of tiny lights that sparkled among cloud effects that gave them the feeling of floating in the sky as Ben Zorren told her that it was his first time in Las Vegas after spending many years abroad. Then over chateaubriand as he flattered her with the typical bullshit of a guy on the make, Gladys flushed with excitement as Frank Sinatra walked over to their table.

"Sorry to interrupt your dinner, Ben. Just wanted to say hello."

Zorren did not know what Sinatra was going to say next, only that whatever it was would effectively quash any chance of screwing the gorgeous woman across the table.

"Aren't you going to introduce me to your lovely lady?"

"Frank, I'd like you to meet Gladys Anderson," he said cautiously, waiting for the other shoe to drop. "Gladys, this is Frank Sinatra."

"Ben is a hell of a guy, Gladys," said Sinatra, taking her hand and kissing it. "Treat him right."

"I can't believe you're friends with Frank Sinatra," said Gladys as she watched the singer lead his party out of the restaurant, sensing that there might be a lot more to her middle-aged Romeo than met the eye.

After dinner, as Gladys and Zorren walked through the casino, she suggested checking out the action at one of the craps tables where players let out a collective groan at a come out roll of snake eyes. It had been a long time since Zorren had been in a dice game, but he knew that luck, good or bad, ran in streaks, so they squeezed into a spot at the end of the table where he put $100 on the Don't Pass line. Winner. And Zorren continued to win as he bet against the dice when they were cold and with the dice when they were hot.

From the bell desk, Freddy recognized the man with long sideburns he had been told to keep an eye out for. He also recognized Gladys and laughed as he saw the man give her a stack of chips with which to bet, though Freddy knew she would palm and stash them in her purse with systematic efficiency. Zorren knew that he was being hustled but didn't care. Whatever it took to get Gladys out of that low-cut dress blue dress. Then after a while Zorren figured he had been generous enough. Could almost feel himself inside her but she wanted to make one more stop.

Liberace sang *Wooly Bully,* Sunny suggestively stroked the microphone as she warbled *California Dreamin'* and Ben Zorren wondered what the hell he was doing at a smoky bowling alley bar where the late-night crowd cheered on the girl he had already dropped a bundle on as she murdered Shirley Bassey's *Goldfinger.* All eyes on Gladys until midway through the song when like a shot people raced from their tables toward the payphone as a shitfaced Howard Hughes, wearing a three-cornered pirate hat, walked in and downed a drink at the bar.

Sunny moved quickly against the tide, spiriting the drunk who didn't measure up out of Buddy Bomar's Bowlarama in the direction of a motel near the end of the Strip where she would fulfill every one of his perverted pirate fantasies. Let loose with cries of enthusiasm as long as the meter was running then, after taking all the cash she could fuck out of this lunatic, would drop a dime and claim the $50,000 reward.

With Hughes again in the wind, Sammy Shake cranked up the Wurlitzer and had everyone back in their seats cheering on Gladys as she gave her song another try. Nobody noticing as the cocktail waitress wrapped a napkin around Howard Hughes's empty glass and put it in her purse.

CHAPTER 21

"The desk clerk at the Six Palms Motel heard screams coming from one of the rooms, so he used his pass key and found a dead hooker with a sword jammed in her pussy and this creep standing over her jerking off," Harry told Dalitz as he hustled the belligerent sicko, pants on backwards and still wearing the three-cornered pirate hat, into the penthouse suite.

"Why the fuck did you make me learn how to walk and talk like Howard Hughes if you're just gonna keep me locked up in this room like a prisoner?" Albert Lee Soames yelled at Dalitz.

"Get up here now!" Dalitz barked into the phone, then slammed down the receiver and looked at Harry. "Did anybody else see this asshole at the motel?"

"The hooker signed the register and snuck him into the room, so even the desk clerk didn't see him until he discovered the murder. That's when he called me."

"Can we trust him to keep his mouth shut?"

"Once we give him his fifty grand reward."

"What about the body?"

"The sheriff and his deputy are out in the desert digging a hole."

"Let me out of here or I'll call the fucking cops!" Soames screamed at Dalitz.

"Don't forget to tell them about the hooker you shish kabobbed."

"They'll give me a pass when I tell them that you killed Howard Hughes and paid me to take his place."

Dalitz slugged him.

Even woozy from the booze, the bennies and the crack in the jaw, the incensed Soames scrambled to his feet. Smashed a lamp and lunged at Dalitz with a jagged piece of porcelain just as two of the Rogers rushed in and broke it up. Kicking and spitting as the hired muscle manhandled him into the other room and slammed him hard onto the bed. One Roger pinning him down as he continued fighting to free himself while Dalitz watched the other remove previously placed items from the nightstand drawer. Bent spoon. Lighter. A length of rubber hose he used to tie him off and find a ripe vein. Drew heroin into a syringe then jabbed the needle in Soames's arm.

"I want a man in this room and another one standing guard in the hall outside the door twenty-four hours a day," ordered Dalitz as the dope quickly took the fight out of the man on the bed. "Nobody in, nobody out, and he doesn't leave your sight for a second. He needs to take a piss, you hold his dick. He takes a shit, you wipe his ass. And if either of you even think about leaving your post before your relief arrives, you won't live to regret it."

After making sure that both Rogers were at their assigned

posts, Dalitz went into the living room and sunk into an armchair across from Harry.

"Everything's under control."

"Is it, Moe?" snapped Harry who had been running on caffeine the past forty-eight hours. Leaning aggressively forward on the sofa, resentful of Dalitz's arrogance but even more so at how he was being used. "You kept me in the dark for months while you had that maniac's face worked on until he looked exactly like Hughes, then killed the real Hughes and made the switch. And even though until recently I didn't know about any of it, you've made me complicit in all of it. So, stop playing me for a sucker. You murdered one of the richest men in America so you could cash in on something big, and I want to know what it is."

"I'm going to steal the $500 million Hughes got from selling TWA."

"That airline deal closed a year ago."

"My man on Wall Street says the cash is still in the bank while he looks for the right investment opportunity, so I created my own Howard Hughes who is going to pay top dollar to buy bust out businesses and shell companies I control until every cent of that TWA money is in my pocket."

Harry lit a Lucky. Sat back and exhaled a stream of smoke as he contemplated the situation.

"I read somewhere a while ago that Hughes was thinking about buying all the empty desert land west of the city so he could test guided missile devices for the government. Move his aircraft company out there, build new neighborhoods and maybe even suburbs. Since he's already on record as being interested, why not sell him worthless land instead of worthless companies? A land deal wouldn't raise any red flags and there would be far fewer legal hoops to jump through."

"Even a lunatic like Hughes wouldn't shell out a fortune for worthless rock and sand."

"You're playing with fire, Moe. Because, dead or alive, Hughes has an entire organization of lawyers and accountants looking after his money and I don't see how you expect to steal half a billion dollars without them smelling a rat."

"They won't suspect a thing, because you are going to sign Hughes's name to a letter offering Bob Maheu the job of facilitating the purchase of all those worthless companies while the great man exiles himself in this penthouse for some much-needed rest."

"The same way we got him to act as go between for the Desert Inn sale?"

"A test run to make sure my TWA plan would work. And because Maheu has a history with Hughes, when you signed Hughes's name on the D.I. sale documents, no one in the organization thought twice about it."

"Nobody questioned it because my forgery of his signature was spot on. And because it was a one-time deal, just as selling Hughes desert land would be a one-time deal."

"I'm not selling him the desert because I don't own the desert. Who does own the fucking desert anyway? Besides, I have a portfolio of dummy companies ready to sell that I do own."

"You're pushing your luck, Moe. What makes you so sure that Maheu won't get suspicious even once while handling the purchase of all those worthless companies?"

"Because he knows Hughes's track record of making deals that seem foolish but later prove to be visionary."

"Even if you're right about all this, that animal in the bedroom won't fool Maheu for a second."

"He won't have to because all communication with Hughes will be done by memo. No calls, no personal contact and he will sign a non-disclosure agreement guaranteeing that all financial dealings remain confidential. None of which will seem even the least bit strange to Maheu because he already knows that Hughes is a nut case, and for a $10,000 a week salary paid in cash he'll never question anything."

"As long as we keep Soames doped-up and out of sight. But eventually somebody in the Hughes organization will wonder why nobody has seen the boss and come around asking questions."

"It will never happen, because Hughes has a history of disappearing for months at a time to build planes, bang broads and whatever the fuck else he does, and the company runs just fine without him. And with all of the diversified investments he has, the company would continue to operate at a profit even if he never came back." Dalitz was confident. Outlined simple logistics. "You will sign Hughes's name to memos of instruction, legal documents and contracts that Maheu will pick up, along with his weekly pay envelope at the casino cage. And you will receive documents he thinks he is leaving for Hughes the same way. Neither of you will ever see the other. It's foolproof."

"It's only foolproof if Maheu continues to believe it's business as usual around here. And that includes keeping

Chandler from poking his fat nose into things."

"Stop looking for problems, Harry. Grabbing that TWA money will be easier than a two dollar whore."

"Then I want the points you promised me in the Desert Inn plus a piece of every dollar you get from selling those worthless businesses." Harry stubbed out his cigarette. "You can't make any of this happen without me."

"We'll talk details later," said Dalitz as he got up and checked himself out in the mirror. Straightened his tie, shot his cuffs and smiled approval at the reflection. "Right now, I have a date with Angie Dickinson."

"We're going to settle this now."

"Did I ever tell you about the magical things that woman can do with her tongue? She's famous for it."

"Quit stalling. We're going to settle this right now or you're on your own."

Dalitz knew that he could not pull off this massive fraud without Harry, but that did not make it any easier for the man who had not shared a dime of profit for decades to suddenly do so now. Knowing that even spending the money like a drunken sailor it would take him more years than he had left to blow through half a billion dollars, but that did not mean it wouldn't be fun to try. Maybe he would take a page from the Mormon playbook and buy every hotel on the Las Vegas Strip, which would still leave enough money left over to buy Palm Springs.

"You should let me set you up with Angie. An afternoon with her will change your life."

"Now, Moe."

Dalitz knew it would be pointless to stall any longer. Also, that after cutting Harry in he would still have enough money left after buying Palm Springs to own a piece of the Dick Nixon White House.

"Help me get Maheu set up and operating smoothly and I'll give you ten percent of everything."

"Twenty."

"I don't have to give you anything."

"And I don't have to sign Hughes's name to anything."

They shook hands at fifteen percent, each man feeling he had gotten the short end of the stick.

CHAPTER 22

"You're ... You're Don Adams," sputtered Charlotte, starstruck inside the lobby of the Desert Inn as Harry shook hands with the comedian who had skyrocketed to fame portraying a bumbling secret agent on the hit television show *Get Smart.*

"Meet my girlfriend, Charlotte. She's your biggest fan."

"What a coincidence," smiled Adams, his eyes zeroing in on her clinging yellow knit mini-dress. "I'm *her* biggest fan."

"Join us for a drink?"

"Next time, Harry. I've got to get back to the Sands for my late show."

The comedian made his exit with a running gag from *Get Smart* as he took Charlotte in his arms and leaned close with a kiss that did not come close to landing.

"Missed it by *that* much."

"Gosh, Harry," said Charlotte as she watched her favorite TV star walk away. "Are there any celebrities you don't know?"

"Not in this town."

The casino was alive with action as one-armed bandits spit

out silver dollars and hot craps shooters rolled sevens. Never off duty, Harry spotted empty glasses at a blackjack table and told a cocktail waitress get over there with refills on the double. Took one more look around to make certain everything was as it should be, then got into the elevator with his long-legged girlfriend who was still blinded by starlight. The music in her smile sending Harry soaring to the outer limits, making him wonder if he had ever really been happy before the day he met Charlotte Kaye.

Charlotte kicked off her heels and got comfortable on Harry's sofa as he dimmed the lights and put his new Ronnie Scott record on the turntable. Together every night for the past week and still her skin tingled as the man she had fallen for set the stage for romance. He brought them each a bottle of Miller High Life as, not being an experienced drinker, she had found the alcohol content of beer to be on par with her level of tolerance. She purred as Harry's fingers caressed her cheek, blinded by a love that had pulled her in so deep that she was oblivious to the consequences. Reached for her purse on the coffee table, then took out a gift-wrapped package and handed it to him.

"What's the occasion?"

"So you'll never forget that first afternoon at Lew's Luncheonette."

He removed the wrapping paper to find a hard cover first edition of *Kiss Me Deadly* signed by Mickey Spillane.

"Where did you get this? Nobody in Vegas sells signed first editions."

"I made some calls to booksellers in New York, and when I

finally located a copy had them send it special delivery."

As pleased as Harry was with the gift, it touched him even more that Charlotte cared enough to seek it out and buy it for him. Was beginning to understand the feeling of loss whenever she walked out of a room and the surge of invincibility when she returned, his stomach turning to jelly as the specks of silver in her eyes danced in seductive light. He knew that love was a big word, so big a word that he had never before even considered saying it to anyone. And as much as his heart prompted him to say it now, he knew it was too soon.

Passion on the sofa swept them into the bedroom where she trembled as Harry eased her out of the yellow dress. Slowly kissed every inch of Charlotte's long naked body until his tongue ignited her orgasm. Switched his position to flip the script but she jerked her head away. Almost as if the thought of having a cock in her mouth repulsed her, a concept foreign to Harry as the girls he usually dated always dove right in. Maybe Charlotte's aversion was due to the inexperience of a small town midwestern upbringing, but whatever it was that turned her off he figured she would eventually come around. If not, it was a small price to pay for the love of a girl who was quickly becoming his everything.

In the morning they wore silk kimonos on the terrace as a room service waiter served eggs Benedict, a dish that was new to Charlotte. First it was pinball, now fellatio and hollandaise sauce, making Harry wonder what century it was in Elkhorn, Wisconsin. He watched her gaze out at men chasing little white balls amid the lush greenery of the Desert Inn golf course, making him feel good to see her enjoy the privileged trappings of a lifestyle he had come to take for granted.

"I bet you're a great golfer," she said.

"I hardly ever play. My job keeps me too busy."

"If I lived on a golf course, I'd play every day." Charlotte gestured to the beautiful homes dotting the perimeter. "Does Howard Hughes live in one of those?"

"Howard lives upstairs."

"Can I meet him?"

"He's reclusive and doesn't leave the penthouse."

"Come on, Harry. You're friends with everybody. Can't we just knock on his door and say hello?"

Harry refilled Charlotte's glass with fresh orange juice, then asked which of the golf course homes she liked the best.

"That big one by the trees with the oval-shaped swimming pool," she said without having to think twice, pointing to a canary yellow contemporary with sleek modern lines. "It's the most fabulous house I've ever seen. Who lives there?"

"I'll find out."

Harry slid his hands inside her kimono and kissed her, then as he led her toward the bedroom for an encore the telephone rang. After a brief conversation, he told Charlotte that there was something downstairs he needed to take care of.

"There's something in the bedroom you need to take care of first."

He picked her up and carried her to the bed.

"Keep it warm. I won't be gone long."

"What's so important it can't wait?"

"I can't tell you that."

"Sorry I asked."

"You know my job requires me to be on call at all hours."

"Forget it, Harry."

The man accustomed to the playboy lifestyle of never having to explain himself felt bad that he had been so blunt. Words to soothe hurt feelings proved elusive so instead, throwing on a sweater and jeans, he spelled out a truth that she would have to learn to accept.

"Every person has a public life, a private life and a secret life. And that secret life has to stay secret."

"Aren't couples supposed to share things?"

"Honestly, Charlotte, I don't have a clue what couples are supposed to do. I've never cared about anyone enough to find out."

"Until now?"

"Until now. That's why I would never ask about your secret life."

Charlotte stiffened.

"What makes you think I have a secret life?"

"Maybe it's just what you do when your door is closed and the lights are out, but it belongs only to you."

"I can understand that."

"Then you're the only woman who ever has."

CHAPTER 23

"Who are you and why have you been stalking Moe Dalitz?"

"What I have to say I'll say only to Moe," stonewalled Ben Zorren. Naked and sweaty with hair dye dripping from his long sideburns as two of the Rogers dragged him out of the steam room at the Desert Inn health club.

"You'll talk to me," Harry told him. "So, I'll ask you one last time. Who are you and what do you want?"

"Fuck off, errand boy."

One of the Rogers punched him hard in the gut.

"Okay, okay," he coughed, doubled up and gasping to regain his wind. "I'm Ben Zorren. I was with Moe in Cleveland."

Harry ordered the Rogers to stand outside the door to keep any hotel guests from coming in, then once they were out of earshot told Zorren to continue.

"I was twenty-two. Fast with the girls and even faster with a gun. Nobody could touch me until one night when me and Moe stuck up Lenny Circo for the cash he just heisted from the Cuyahoga Loan Company. Long story short, Moe plugged

Lenny twice in the chest and in the scramble to get the fuck out of there lost his gun. He got away clean, but two days later the cops grabbed me with some of the heist money and pinned the murder on me."

"That's *your* story. How would Moe tell it?"

"I rotted for thirty years in a six by nine cell while Moe was out here getting rich. And now I want to be paid for every one of those thirty years."

"Because he got away and you were stupid enough to get caught?"

"The cops knew it was Dalitz who pulled the trigger on that bum Circo, but he beat the rap because they couldn't find the gun or his share of the money."

"What's your point?" Harry demanded, then threw Zorren a towel. "And cover up before you make me sick."

"My point is *I have that gun,*" Zorren said, all-of-a-sudden feeling he had the upper hand as he wrapped the towel around himself. "I hid it and after thirty years it was still where I stashed it, a .38 caliber revolver that has Moe's prints all over it."

"Where is it?"

"I'll tell you when Dalitz gives me $3 million."

"I hear you've been making time with a showgirl at the Stardust. That takes money, and I'm guessing you don't have much left."

"Moe's not going to buy me off cheap. He owes me every cent of that $3 million for not ratting him out. I did *his* time."

"No, you didn't. You were involved in a homicide that occurred during the commission of a robbery, and that makes you just as guilty as if you had pulled the trigger. Which I'm sure your lawyer told you at the time or you would have tried to save yourself by giving up the gun and ratting out Moe. So, do yourself a favor and get as far away from Vegas as you can, because there is no future in trying to shake down Moe Dalitz."

"$3 million comes out to a $100,000 a year. $8,333 a month and $273 a day."

"And it probably took you all thirty years to figure that out."

"Want to know what it comes to for each second?"

"Nobody cares."

"Dalitz had better care. He has quite the set up out here in Las Vegas, but he won't have it much longer unless he comes across with what he owes me."

"I'll talk to him and let you know what he says."

CHAPTER 24

"Apparently $10,000 in cash every week does guarantee that Maheu won't rock the boat," Harry told Dalitz who munched on a Reuben sandwich as they had a late lunch in the Desert Inn coffee shop. "The first deal memo I signed passed muster all down the line."

"How long until I get my money?"

"There's still more paperwork including signing the final contract, as even Hughes can't push too hard to close the purchase of a worthless company without sending up red flags all over the place."

"What red flags? It's a simple straightforward deal that should have closed days ago."

"You've masked your ownership of Allied Machine Parts through cut outs and dummy corporations," said Harry as he crushed crackers into a bowl of clam chowder. "That slows down the process."

"I want that TWA money, Harry."

"You'll get it, Moe. But you have to understand that pulling off a swindle this big takes time, and this is just the first step.

Then once we close Allied, we can push through bigger deals with far less scrutiny."

"Stop dragging your feet and get me my fucking money." Dalitz took a sip of coffee then nibbled on a French fry. "Now tell me what else has been going on. Anything important I need to know about?"

"Not a thing, Moe. Just business as usual."

"I heard you had to get rough with somebody in the steam room this morning."

"Nothing for you to be concerned about. I took care of it"

"Should I be concerned that you met with the sheriff right afterward?"

"Are you having me followed? Because if you don't trust me after everything we've been through, we can call it quits right now."

"Don't get your bowels in an uproar. Somebody saw that red Corvette of yours parked in front of the sheriff station."

"I was fixing my girl's parking tickets."

"How are things going with that new broad of yours? Word is half the showgirls on the Strip are wearing out their vibrators because you're out of circulation."

Mugshots and a fingerprint card dropped onto the table between them.

"Albert Lee Soames," said Cliff Chandler as he slid uninvited into the booth and faced Dalitz. "A petty thief and narcotics user who, in his entire adult life, has never been out of jail more than a year before being thrown back in. Then several months ago he dropped out of sight. No record of him in any jail, hospital or morgue, which makes me think he had plastic surgery to change his appearance."

"You interrupted my lunch to tell me about some hood who changed his face?"

"When the man you passed off to the media as Howard Hughes went on his two-day drinking spree, he left fingerprints on cocktail glasses everywhere he went." Chandler pointed to the card on the table. "Those fingerprints. Which proves that the man upstairs in the penthouse is not Howard Hughes. It's Albert Lee Soames."

"It doesn't prove shit. Just the prints of some gonif you could have gotten anywhere."

"You killed Hughes and made the switch."

"Prove it, cockroach," snarled Dalitz, his eyes skewering Chandler with a naked hatred.

"I have enough evidence to get the district attorney to ask a judge to issue a writ of habeas corpus forcing you to produce Howard Hughes. The real Howard Hughes. And we both know you can't do that."

"Would he be asking Judge Mowbray, whose kids swim in the backyard pool I paid for? Or Judge Hancock, whose ranch I just paid off?"

"I'll turn every courthouse in Nevada upside down if I have to until I find an honest judge who *will* issue a writ of habeas corpus."

"Tell Vernon White this cheap trick won't work."

"White has nothing to do with this. This is *my* deal and, may the Lord strike me dead if I'm lying, this is definitely not a trick" He locked eyes with Dalitz. "So, you had better listen closely when I tell you that unless you back out of the agreement to sell the Desert Inn to that phony in the penthouse before the sale is approved by the Gaming Commission on Friday morning, and sell the hotel to me, a writ will be issued that will undoubtedly lead to your arrest on charges of fraud and murder."

Dalitz sprinkled salt on his fries, then unscrewed the top of the shaker and dumped the rest of it on the mugshots and fingerprint cards.

"I told you before," Chandler said. "It's a new era in Las Vegas and there is no place for you here anymore. And you, of all people, should know that fingerprints don't lie. So, if you are even half as smart as you think you are, you'll see that this is your last chance to stay out of jail. You have until Friday."

Harry pushed away his soup. No longer hungry as he watched Chandler walk out of the restaurant clutching evidence that could sink them.

"Are you finally convinced that this guy is *never* going to go away? With or without a writ, he's going to find a way inside the penthouse and prove that Soames is a phony. We need to move him somewhere where Chandler will never find him."

Dalitz finished the last bite of his sandwich.

"I know just the place."

CHAPTER 25

"That's deep enough," Dalitz told the deputy who heaved shovelfuls of desert subsoil out of a hole beside a lone Joshua tree.

"Why are we out here, Moe?" Harry wanted to know as the sun began to rise over a vast nothingness of dirt and rock miles from nowhere. Curious as to why a man always careful to ensure at least one degree of separation would take such an unnecessary risk.

"Watch and learn."

Harry watched the deputy climb out of the hole. Watched early morning light reflect off the sheriff's mirrored aviators. Watched Albert Lee Soames who was so doped up he could not tell if it was sunshine or moonlight beaming down on him. Watched the time as he knew that Cliff Chandler's deadline was about to pass and that all the writs in the world could no longer expose their fraud. But Harry did not understand what lesson could possibly be learned by standing witness to an execution.

The sheriff wrapped three shotgun shells in a gasoline-soaked bandana and shoved it into the mouth of the junkie who had outlived his usefulness. Dalitz lit a cigarette then flicked the match at the guest of honor. Panic in Soames's eyes. Pissing himself as the bandana caught fire. Muffled screams of terror as the flame crackled and scorched his skin, followed by an explosion that obliterated the head of the man who had masqueraded as Howard Hughes and toppled the dead ringer into the hole.

Harry threw up. Even the hard-boiled sheriff was nauseous. But Moe Dalitz reveled in the spectacle he had choreographed, then pulled a .357 magnum from his waistband and shot the deputy who fell backward into the hole on top of the headless junkie.

"What the fuck!" screamed the sheriff.

"When Soames was on his bender, you told me that I didn't pay you shitkickers enough to justify the secrets you keep."

"I won't say a word. You know I'm loyal."

Dalitz pointed his gun at the sheriff.

"You should have known better than to try to shake me down, Ralph."

"We're friends, Moe. Think of everything we've done together."

"There you go again. Reminding me that you know where all the bodies are buried."

"That's not what I meant. I won't say anything. You have my word of honor."

"What's the going rate for the word of honor of a corrupt sheriff?"

"I'll do anything you want. For free, as long as I'm in office," pleaded the terrified lawman, backing away until he was up against his truck. "Please, Moe! Put the gun down! Please, Moe! I'm begging you!"

The shot cracked through the desert stillness as the sheriff dropped to the ground. Then, realizing he wasn't hit, rose to his knees and saw two halves of a rattlesnake at the foot of the Joshua tree.

Dalitz looked at the cowering lawman. Lowered the gun.

"Thank you, Moe." The sheriff slumped with relief. "Thank you. You won't regret it."

"I know that, Ralph."

Dalitz put a bullet through the sheriff's aviator sunglasses, then took the truck key from his pocket and kicked him into the hole.

"Never leave any loose ends," Dalitz told Harry. "The Rogers thought they were guarding the real Howard Hughes, so now you and I are the only ones who know the truth about Albert Lee Soames."

Lesson learned.

Harry's qualms about violence were now a moot point as these three murders had pushed him past the point of no return. But on the positive side, Harry knew that it was better to be lucky than good, and right now felt that he was both. Confident in the advantage he had gained by having gotten everything he needed to further his personal agenda at the sheriff station the day before.

"Shovel that dirt back in the hole," Dalitz told him. "We have a funeral to go to."

CHAPTER 26

A warm breeze wafted through the cemetery as a who's who of the casino industry watched a coffin containing the remains of Marie Taxitolo being lowered into the ground. Then as final eulogies were spoken and the gathering began to disperse, Harry stepped away. Reached into the pocket of his double-breasted blue suit and pulled out a cigarette as Moe Dalitz said his goodbyes to the family.

"A beautiful service. Don't you agree, Mr. Lake?" The man whose dark eyes were magnified by tortoise shell glasses extended his hand. "My name is Vernon White, and I believe it would be to our mutual benefit if we became friends."

"Your pal Cliff Chandler wanted to be my friend, but it came with a price tag."

"My friendship is yours at no obligation."

"It's not even noon and I've already had a long day, so if you've got something to say, spit it out."

"You are well respected in the business community and all indications point to the fact that you are an honorable man, which makes me curious as to why you pledge allegiance to a man who is not loyal to you."

"Save the sermon."

"Your boss is not loyal to his wife. Not loyal to anyone he has ever done business with, and if Sid Klein were here, he could attest to the fact that he is not even loyal to his best friends. His commitment goes no further than the man in the mirror, which means that once he has extracted from you everything he needs he will stick a knife in your back. Possibly literally."

"I can take care of myself, White."

"Perhaps that's true for the moment, but a young man like yourself needs to look toward the future because the longer you associate yourself with a gangster like Morris Dalitz, the greater the chance you will become Morris Dalitz."

"I know exactly what my future holds and will do whatever it takes to get everything I want. *Whatever it takes* and nobody is going to stop me. Not you, not Chandler. Nobody."

"That's telling him, Harry," punctuated Dalitz as he walked up and joined them. "And you can stop pitching, White. The Gaming Commission approved the sale of the Desert Inn to Howard Hughes two hours ago."

"I'm told that approval was granted even though Mr. Hughes was under the weather and unable to attend the meeting."

"He had a headache, like you're starting to give me. Don't you think it's disrespectful to show up here and try to make a move while I'm paying final respects to a dear friend?"

"It is for that very reason I feel the setting to be apropos, Morris. Because, as Mrs. Taxitolo braved the pain of her final days in the cancer ward, Catholic guilt demanded that she cleanse her soul in order to get into heaven, so she wrote a death bed confession in which she admitted to marital indiscretion with you."

"I fucked Charlie Taxi's wife. So, what?"

"One of the evils of alcohol is that it loosens lips, as evidenced by one evening at a cocktail party where Mrs. Taxitolo confessed her infidelity to some of the other wives and it was not long before all of the dirty laundry was aired." Vernon White pushed his glasses back on the bridge of his nose, then removed a folded piece of paper from the inside pocket of his suit coat. "This is a photostat of her death bed confession. I, of course, have the original secured in a safe place."

"How did you get your hands on it?"

"She entrusted a nurse to deliver this letter to her priest, but as a devout member of the Mormon faith the angel of mercy instead gave it to me."

"Why should I give two shits about any of this?"

"Because along with confession of her own infidelity, Mrs. Taxitolo included details of your dalliances with spouses of other prominent men including the governor's wife. And how each of them had acquiesced to your carnal advances only after you had threatened to harm their husbands."

"The broad was doped up on pain medication. Nobody's going to take what she wrote seriously."

"What about Sam Giancana, who has a well-documented reputation as a gangster who other gangsters fear? How long do you think you will remain alive once he reads the letter and discovers that you had your way with his girlfriend Phyllis McGuire?"

"If you're offering to give me the letter in exchange for getting Hughes to sell the D.I. to that putz Chandler, you can go fuck yourself."

"Cliff Chandler is no longer affiliated with my bid to acquire the Desert Inn."

"Your bid, huh? I should have figured that there was too much money involved for you not to screw the church by going rogue and trying to take it all for yourself." Dalitz laughed loudly, drawing looks from the mourners who remained. "The funny part now will be watching you two bozos trying to fuck each other out of a hotel that neither one of you will ever own."

"You would be wise not to underestimate me."

"And you would be wise not to underestimate Chandler, because that cockroach is not going to go away quietly."

"I have already laid the groundwork to silence Brother Cliff."

"The only way you can be sure of that is to dig a hole."

"Our methods may differ, Morris, but trust me when I say that the end result will be the same. You have my personal guarantee that after tonight Cliff Chandler will never bother you again."

"But you're not going to stop bothering me, are you?"

"I do not care who signs Howard Hughes's name on the dotted line as long as I receive title to the property. Arrange for the Desert Inn to be legally sold to me or a lot of powerful men will become aware of a dying woman's final words. Leaving you ostracized with nowhere to turn. A pariah in a town you take credit for building, left with nothing except to ponder your own final words."

"I can handle those stuffed shirts."

"I very much doubt it, but for the sake of argument let's assume that's true. Then imagine how Sam Giancana will react when he reads this," said Vernon White as he handed Dalitz the photostat of Marie Taxitolo's death bed confession. "I suggest you waste no time in arranging the sale."

As he watched Vernon White walk to his car, Dalitz knew that he was no longer sparring with some putz turning the courthouse upside down searching for an honest judge he would never find. Knew that Marie Taxitolo's letter was dynamite, and White held a lit match. Knew that, as boss of the Chicago Outfit, Sam Giancana had rigged ballot boxes that gave Kennedy the White House in 1960, only to help mastermind his assassination three years later when JFK failed to honor his end of the bargain. And, most importantly, Moe Dalitz knew that any man powerful enough to murder the President of the United States would not think twice before putting a bullet in his head if he suspected that he had even winked at Phyllis McGuire.

CHAPTER 27

The teenage girl was blond and very pretty. The cock in her mouth was rock hard.

"This picture is a fake!" thundered an enraged Cliff Chandler as he ripped up the compromising image of his daughter.

"I can assure you the photograph is quite authentic," Vernon White stated calmly as the former allies faced off in the living room of his expansive ranch-style home. "Also, that I possess additional copies as well as the negative."

"It's a damn fake!"

"You were warned that consequences would be extreme if you did not confine your business activity to selling automobiles."

"May I serve you a glass of lemonade, Mr. Chandler?" offered Della White, a soft-spoken middle-aged woman wearing a matronly black dress and pearls as she knitted on the sofa. "Or maybe a Sanka?"

Chandler paced the room, building up a head of steam.

"Annie is a lovely girl, Cliff, and you are to be commended

for doing a splendid job of raising her to honor and obey the Lord. And as it is I who represents the Lord in Las Vegas, she was quite eager to obey me."

"That's a lie! My Annie would never do anything like that."

"Your Annie paid a steep price for her father alerting Morris Dalitz to the fact that we were aware of Albert Lee Soames."

"I'm the one who discovered the identity of Soames. Not you. How do you even know about him?"

"Don't be so naïve as to believe that there is anything you do of which I am not aware. Your ill-advised power play allowed Dalitz the opportunity to mount a proactive defense that undoubtedly resulted in the demise of the imposter the same way your arrogance led to the untimely death of Sid Klein."

"We don't know for sure that Soames is dead."

"Again, you are being naïve."

"Then I'll find another way to prove that the Desert Inn sale was fraudulent."

"What is it going to take to get you to stand down, Cliff? Why do you continue to insist upon discovering the hard way just how far I will go to get what I want?"

Vernon White removed the handkerchief from his pocket and brushed a bit of dust from an ivory carving of Jesus Christ that centered a sweeping spiritual display that drew focus from everywhere in the room, then turned to his wife who reached into her knitting basket and handed him several more photographs.

"I'm particularly fond of this one," White smiled, then handed it to his guest.

"I'll fucking kill you!" raged Chandler as he eyed the explicit photograph of Vernon White engaged in sexual intercourse with his teenage daughter.

"No, you won't. Because murder is the one unforgivable sin that will prevent you from sitting at the foot of the Lord in everlasting glory."

"You raped my daughter!"

"On the contrary, Cliff. You can see in sharp focus that she quite enjoyed our sexual encounter."

Chandler threw the photograph at White, then yelled at his wife. "And you! How can you condone this?"

"Let me bring you a nice cup of Sanka," Della again offered, then put down her knitting. "It will calm you down."

"You probably took the pictures. You're as perverted as he is."

"God allows my husband the polygamous option of marrying these young girls, but he respects me by not making them a permanent part of our life. And he respects them by preserving their virginity."

"Girls? Plural?"

"It's true that I allow most of them to service me in ways that preserve their innocence." White picked the photo up off the floor and looked at it fondly. "But, as you can see, I penetrated your daughter in such a way that she will be forever ruined for any decent man."

Chandler collapsed onto a chair, feeling as if the life had been beaten out of him by the man who was supposed to represent God in Las Vegas yet was nothing more than a pervert who represented the vilest evil.

"You won't get away with it, White. I'm going to make sure that the leadership in Salt Lake knows all about the unconscionable crimes you've committed in the name of the church."

"I explained to you before that the Quorum of the Twelve Apostles allow me great latitude in order to achieve desired results."

"I'm sure that latitude doesn't extend to the raping of young girls."

"These girls give themselves freely for the greater good."

"They don't *give* anything. Their innocence is stolen from them and the greater good is nothing but black ink on a ledger sheet."

"The church is like any other business in that it needs to generate a profit. And being a businessman yourself, I am sure you understand that it is often necessary to go above and beyond in order to increase the bottom line."

"I never raped a cheerleader to sell a Camaro."

"Be that as it may, evidence has come into my possession that will leave Morris Dalitz with no choice but to sell me the Desert Inn. So, listen very carefully when I tell you that if you again go anywhere near the man before or after I assume ownership of the hotel, sexually explicit photographs of your daughter will be made public. Do you understand?"

"For the first time in my life I understand everything." Chandler stood and faced his adversary. "Seeing the unconscionable things you are capable of has opened my eyes so that, rather than blindly taking the church's word for it, I can now see the real difference between right and wrong. How the ugliness in you contrasts the beauty of treating people the way I would like them to treat me, and I will pray for the Lord to give me guidance of how to stay true to that belief as I search for a way to destroy you while at the same time protecting my little girl."

"That is a threat you will live to regret."

"My only regret is that I should have listened when the devil behind the horseshoe desk said that both you and the Mormon church were nothing more than a bunch of racketeers."

CHAPTER 28

"You're Jewish, right? I can always tell. Bald, heavy set and a hook nose that's sucking up your lip," shot Don Rickles from the stage of the Casbar Lounge at the Sahara Hotel. "And what are you laughing at, lady? You're the only one with a mink stole and it's 105 in here. You're either a Jew or an old brown beaver in heat."

As the short balding comedian sweating through his tuxedo continued to bombard the audience with insults, his eyes locked onto a pretty blonde seated ringside.

"Does the vice squad know you're back in town? You still do that trick with the horse?" He watched the girl flush with embarrassment. "Just kidding, sweetheart. What's your name?"

"Charlotte."

"Stand up, Charlotte. Let's get a good look at you."

Wives gave a sharp elbow to husbands whose eyes locked a bit too long on the leggy stunner in the tight flowery dress.

"That's my kind of broad. I love a tall broad." Rickles gave her a lecherous look, then paused a moment and shrugged.

"You waiting for me to throw you a basketball? Sit back down with your queer boyfriend."

Audiences loved the comic's rubber-tipped zingers, and this night was no different as the show ended with a standing ovation led by the old brown beaver in heat. And as the lounge emptied, Harry and Charlotte hung around at the bar.

"The Sahara hasn't announced it yet, but Rickles is about to sign the biggest contract ever for a lounge performer. $4 million over three years for insulting people."

"My Uncle Ammon does it for free."

"I though you didn't have any family."

"I meant *did*. He died a few years ago."

As the bartender brought two beers and Harry lit a Lucky, Charlotte asked him how old he was when he started smoking.

"Eleven. Two packs a day since I was fourteen."

"Seriously, Harry. How old were you?"

"Eleven. I grew up in a cigar store."

"Why can't you ever give me a straight answer when I ask about growing up in New York? Do you have any brothers and sisters? Tell me about your parents. What are their names?"

"Charles and Patricia. They died when I was ten."

"I'm sorry, Harry." Then seeing sadness cloud his eyes, Charlotte slammed the brakes on her curiosity and removed a cigarette from his pack. "Teach me to smoke."

Harry laughed at the absurdity of the request.

"What's so funny? Every woman in Las Vegas smokes."

Harry thought back twenty years to when Bug Eyed Bennie flicked his Zippo and told him, "Just smoke the fucking thing". Then took a more obliging tack by instructing her to hold a match to the end of the cigarette and slowly breathe in.

Charlotte did. Charlotte coughed.

"Draw in just a little bit of smoke, hold it in your mouth for a moment then let it out."

No cough this time.

"Keep doing that until you get used to it."

The smoke made her eyes water, but she began to feel comfortable with the cigarette between her fingers.

"Now try it again, this time letting some of the smoke into your lungs. Then blow it out."

Charlotte mastered it but didn't like it. Stubbed the butt out in an ashtray then cooled her throat with a sip of beer.

"You're a hell of a looker, Stretch," said Rickles, face still shiny with perspiration from the stage lights as he walked over and joined them. "You can do a lot better than this bum."

"Like you, maybe?"

"I like a sassy broad. Treat her right, Harry, or I'll steal her away from you."

"Nobody is ever going to take this woman away from me."

"That's what *you* say." Rickles looked playfully at Charlotte. "Listen, Stretch. When this queer disappoints you in bed later, just give him the manual so he can see what he left out."

"And if that doesn't work, I'll call you," Charlotte smiled.

"God, I love this broad!" Rickles swooned. "I'm serious, Harry. Treat her right or I'll steal her away from you."

"Join us for a drink?"

"Thanks, Harry. But I've got two more shows to do."

As they watched the funny man walk away and disappear

backstage, Charlotte noticed that Harry all-of-a-sudden seemed preoccupied.

"Are you thinking about your parents?"

"In a way."

"How did they die? Was it a car accident?"

"They were murdered."

"Oh, Harry." She placed her hand on his, then was hit with a horrible thought. "You didn't see it happen, did you?"

"No."

"And you didn't really grow up in a cigar store."

"I ran away from the foster home and the man who owned the cigar store took me in, made me go to school and taught me how to deal with the pain I felt from losing my parents. How did you deal with losing your parents?"

"Moved on with my life the best I could." She squeezed his hand. "Charles and Patricia must have been wonderful people for you to hold onto their memory so strongly."

"Even though I was just a little kid I knew how much in love my parents were, and I've searched my entire life for a woman who would look at me the way my mom looked at my dad."

Even in the dimly lit lounge Harry could see that same look in Charlotte's eyes. Leaned close and kissed her until there was no doubt in his mind. Told her that he loved her, and Charlotte's heart melted.

"I love you too, Harry," she said, wrapping her arms securely around the man she would never let get away. "But you really weren't thinking about your parents before, were you? You've been preoccupied about something else all evening. Are you worried that you're going to lose your job now that Howard

Hughes owns the Desert Inn?"

"I can't go into details, but I have a once-in-a-lifetime opportunity that is either going to make me or break me and I can't afford to lose focus."

"Break you how? You're scaring me."

"I never should have said anything."

"You're not in danger, are you? Because I've heard stories that Moe Dalitz used to be a gangster."

Involvement in the murders of Sid Klein, Albert Lee Soames, the sheriff and deputy, even though peripheral, made Harry feel like *he* was a gangster. Forgery and fraud confirmed it. Fearful that becoming more and more like Dalitz would lead to a shame he could never overcome. Then again seeing that look in Charlotte's eyes, he began to feel confident that over time her love would wash away every dirty bit of Moe Dalitz that had ever stuck to him.

"When this deal pays off, I'll be able to tell you everything about everything. So please bear with me a little longer, Charlotte, and I promise that there will be no more secrets and to you my entire life will be an open book."

Illuminated by a zillion watts of neon, the cool desert night was invigorating as Harry and his lady walked hand in hand past the Riviera, then crossed the street to the Stardust. Past giant Easter Island stone carvings that stood sentry in front of Aku Aku, a Polynesian restaurant and bar that made Charlotte feel as if she had been transported to the South Seas. Forgoing beer they kept with the theme by ordering exotic tiki cocktails from a waitress in a slinky sarong, then Harry looked at his watch and shook a cigarette out of his pack and offered it to his girl.

"I think one was enough for me."

"Maybe it's time for me to quit, too," he said, firing up the Lucky. "I don't get any enjoyment out of smoking anymore. Nothing but a habit."

She noticed him again check his watch.

"I'm sorry, Charlotte, but I have to see someone in the casino. It's business and I'll only be a couple minutes."

"Take your time," she said, already feeling the rum wallop of her Bora Bora Squeeze as she embraced the promise that her man's secret life would soon become an open book.

Harry walked out of the bar and made his way backstage at the Lido de Paris showroom where the dancers were changing out of their costumes. He was the king of midnight, and every time he walked into a dressing room of half-naked women, would walk out with at least one on his arm. But that was before Charlotte, and tonight he really was backstage on business. Found Gladys sitting topless in front of a makeup mirror and asked about her relationship with Ben Zorren.

"Has he fallen for you?"

"That's a stupid question," Gladys grinned as she squeezed her tits.

"How do you feel about him?"

"He's not much to look at and I think he's running short of cash, so I'm going to cut him loose."

"Don't." Harry handed her a large roll of bills. "I want you to stay with him a while longer."

CHAPTER 29

Charlotte looked great a tight T-shirt and cut-offs as she glided past sunbathers at the Bali Hai pool, a spring in her step because the night before her man had said those three magic words. A bag of groceries wedged in the crook of her arm as she passed through the resort motel's tropical gardens, marveling as she always did that such lush greenery could thrive so magnificently in the desert. Nodded hello to a neighbor then slid her key into the lock and pushed open the door to her room. Then dropped the bag, a bottle of orange juice shattering on the floor.

"How did you get in here?" she demanded of the man sitting on her bed.

"Why have you have been avoiding me, Charlotte?"

"Because I'm through with you," she said as she grabbed a bath towel and began to clean up the mess. "I'm through with all of it, so get out of here and don't ever come back."

"You look especially sexy today," he smiled, eyes hugging her thin cotton shirt as he patted the bed. "Come and sit next to me."

"This is close enough," she said as she put the last pieces of broken glass into the trash, then parked herself on a chair across the room from Vernon White. "And I mean it. I'm finished with you for good."

"Your mission was to utilize the physical gifts the Lord has blessed you with to obtain useful information from Harry Lake, not to fall in love with him."

"I told you everything I could find out about Howard Hughes."

"You told me nothing I had not already read in the newspaper."

"I'm through doing your dirty work. Harry is a wonderful man and I'm not going to do anything else that might hurt him."

Vernon White removed his navy-blue blazer and laid it carefully on the bed beside him.

"And don't get any ideas." She wrapped her hand around a heavy ashtray on the dresser. "Just because you've been molesting me since I was thirteen doesn't mean I won't smash your face in if you ever put your disgusting hands on me again. It all ends now."

"I admire spirit in a young woman but make no mistake that you will continue to do exactly as you are told, or the church will see to it that your father loses his job and that your entire family is excommunicated and ostracized by the community." There was no mistaking the power behind the threat. "Then consider how your Mr. Lake will react when he finds out that you are not an innocent girl from Wisconsin but a Mormon operative from Provo, Utah, and that everything you have told him since the moment you met has been a lie for the purpose of sabotaging his business interests. I'm certain I need not remind you that gangsters have a particularly cold-blooded way of dealing with betrayal."

"Harry is *not* a gangster."

"It should be obvious that the only way you can protect yourself and your family is to beg the Lord's forgiveness and follow my direction until you have successfully completed your mission."

"Get it through your thick head that I'm through spying for you."

"What have you overheard about a man named Bob Maheu?"

"I told you I'm through."

"He is an occasional associate of Howard Hughes who has been seen at the Desert Inn the past few days." Vernon White showed her a photograph of Bob Maheu. "Have you seen him with Morris Dalitz or with Mr. Lake?"

It became obvious to Charlotte that White had her backed into a corner where the only way to keep the man she loved was to betray the man she loved. Where the only way to protect her family was to betray herself.

"I need you to keep your eyes and ears open. Search for any paperwork or phone messages naming Mr. Maheu or Mr. Hughes."

"I'll make you a deal." She got up from her chair, feeling that forcing him to look up at her might provide a psychological advantage. "I will get you the information about Bob Maheu if you agree that afterwards you will leave me and my family alone, and that we will never see each other again."

"I could not in good conscience enter into any agreement that would keep us apart, dear Charlotte. Ours is a bond that can never be broken."

"Think again, creep. Because I'm breaking it right now."

"I caution you not to act in haste."

"It's over!"

Vernon White picked up the telephone.

"Then you leave me with no choice but to provide Mr. Lake with all of the salacious details of how much you enjoy getting on your knees and providing me oral pleasure."

"Even you couldn't be that cruel."

"After speaking with Mr. Lake, I shall then telephone your father and tell him that he does not need to report for work tomorrow. Or ever again."

"He'll find another job."

"Not in Utah."

"What kind of monster gets his kicks destroying another person's family?"

"I want to know the reason Bob Maheu has been spending time at the Desert Inn, and I want that information quickly. Not just the headlines. I want every detail." Vernon White loosened his belt then lowered his trousers and underwear. "Now get on about the business of doing what you do best."

She averted her eyes from the veiny middle-aged cock that had made her want to puke since she was in the seventh grade.

"Shall I telephone your father?"

Charlotte got down on her knees.

CHAPTER 30

Charlotte searched Harry's closet, checking the pockets of his jackets and suits but came up empty. Nothing in the writing desk or in the nightstands, but why would there be, as any documentation or correspondence naming Bob Maheu or Howard Hughes would certainly be kept at his office. But just in case, while her man was in the shower she continued to look, opening a dresser drawer, careful not to move his ties even an inch. Sock drawer. Underwear drawer. Then as the water shut off, she pushed shut his sweater drawer, fear shooting through her as she saw Harry watching her in the mirror.

Dripping wet he walked toward her, then Charlotte exhaled a sigh of relief as he reached around to unzip her emerald gown.

"You look amazing."

"It took me an hour to look this amazing," she said, pulling away. "Now hurry up, Harry, or we'll be late."

"Who wants to listen to a bunch of squares talk about politics when we can go back to bed and order room service?"

"I thought you wanted to go to this party."

"I'm obligated to make an appearance." His eyes X-rayed her gown. "But we can cut out before the speeches."

Charlotte noticed the sleeve of a sweater sticking out of a dresser drawer. Turned so that Harry's attention would follow her in the other direction.

"Then go dry off and put on your tux. Because the sooner we get there the sooner we can leave and get back to bed."

Harry got dressed. Charlotte straightened the drawer. Then a half hour later the lovebirds were mixing with VIPs at a black-tie fundraiser for U.S. Senator Howard Cannon. Mayor Gragson was there. *Las Vegas Sun* editor Hank Greenspun, Jerry Lewis and Elvis Pressley. Even mobster Johnny Rosselli made the scene, as the politician had not been born who cared how dirty the money was.

Harry and Charlotte noshed canapes, sipped champagne and danced the twist as on the bandstand Louis Prima powered through *Jump, Jive and Wail.* Then she turned pale as a sheet as Vernon White entered the ballroom flanked by two imposing men dressed in matching pearl-gray suits. Began to shake as White left his muscle by the door and wove his way through the partygoers in their direction.

"What's wrong?" said Harry, gripping Charlotte's shoulders to steady her.

"Can we get out of here? Right now. Please, I'm going to be sick."

As they made a hasty exit, Vernon White approached Moe Dalitz, who had been holding court near them. A bright smile on White's face but hostility cut sharply through the veneer.

"The hoodlums you sent to burglarize my home made such a mess it took my wife most of the day to clean it up. With so much at stake, did you really think I would be naïve enough to keep Marie Taxitolo's letter at such an unsecure location?"

"Did you really think I would sit still and let you blackmail me?"

"There is only one way you will ever gain possession of that letter, Morris, and I strongly suggest that you arrange the Desert Inn sale quickly, as my patience is rapidly approaching its limit."

"Go fuck yourself."

"I don't believe we've met," smiled an attractive woman in a peach Balenciaga gown as she walked up and introduced herself. "I'm Averill Dalitz."

"My name is Vernon White, Mrs. Dalitz. It is an honor to make your acquaintance."

"Are you here with your wife, Mr. White?"

"I am afraid she had a rather exhausting day that required her to remain at home and rest."

"I'm sorry to hear that. Maybe soon the four of us can get together for dinner."

"We would be delighted, Mrs. Dalitz."

"Please, call me Averill. Would you like to dance?"

"I don't think Mormons are allowed to dance," laughed Dalitz.

"What a pity," she said, then flitted away in search of another twist partner.

"Your wife is a beautiful woman," White told Dalitz. "I wonder how many men she is sleeping with."

"How man wives do you have, White?"

"Just one."

"Interesting."

CHAPTER 31

A fat man in a pit-stained guayabera shirt scribbled notes on a *Racing Form* at the Winners Circle bar next to Churchill Downs, then asked the bartender who he liked to win the next race at Gulfstream Park.

"I'm down on Red Lightning."

"That nag couldn't beat a one-legged goldfish."

"Then we're even, because the last horse you gave me is still running."

At the other end of the dark bar Ben Zorren grew angrier by the minute as he nursed a beer, eyes fixed on the door.

"Is that clock right?" Zorren demanded of the bartender.

The guardian of the booze checked his watch, then the Schlitz clock on the wall.

"12:15 any way you look at it. Want another beer?"

"Whiskey."

12:20. 12:30. Zorren watched the door. 12:45. Another shot of whiskey. 1:00. His anger festering. Had to pee but would not take his eyes off the door. Then at 1:10 a beam of sunlight shot into the room as the door was pushed open.

"How they hangin', Harry?" chirped the fat man. "Who do you like in the eighth at Gulfstream?"

"Haven't you learned by now that horses have no respect for a man's bankroll?"

"Then why've you got a *Racing Form* under your arm?"

"Newspaper," Harry said as he held up a folded *Review-Journal.*

"What'll it be, Harry?" asked the bartender.

"Bottle of Miller."

Zorren seethed as he watched the man he had been waiting for make small talk and joke with the bartender. Was about to break it up when Harry walked over to him.

"You're more than an hour late."

"I'm here now."

"You have the money?"

"You have the gun?"

"Not until I see my $3 million."

"$3 million is too much."

"How much will Moe pay?"

Harry shook out a Lucky Strike and took his time lighting it.

"Come on, Lake. How much? $2 million?"

Harry gestured downward.

"One? I won't take less than a million."

"Not a penny."

Zorren grabbed him by the collar and Harry pushed him away.

"Just because you were stupid enough to get thrown into prison does not give you the right to come around here with your hand out."

"If I give that gun to the Cleveland cops, they'll lock Moe up for thirty years. And we both know that old man doesn't have thirty years."

"If you really think the gun is worth something, put an ad in the paper," scoffed Harry as he opened his *Review-Journal* to the classified section, tossed it on the bar and walked out.

As an enraged Ben Zorren yelled at the bartender for another shot of whiskey, a full-page ad caught his attention.

CHAPTER 32

"Feast your eyes on this low-milage palomar red '63 Impala Super Sport, fully loaded with a 283 cubic inch engine and 195 horsepower," pitched Cliff Chandler, smiling into the camera as he and his bulldog Cliff, Jr. shot a commercial in the lot at his dealership. "But you had better get down here fast because this beauty won't last long at the low, low price of only $999. That's right folks, at $999 I'm practically giving this car away. No money down and easy monthly payments of only ... CUT! Darn it, Junior."

Chandler yelled for someone to clean up the massive steaming shit his dog had unloaded on his cowboy boot. Then after a few minutes they started filming again from the top, got through it in one take and Junior followed dutifully as the car dealer went inside to his office and found Ben Zorren sitting behind his desk.

"Get out of my chair."

Zorren leaned back, folded his hands behind his head and smiled. "You've made some big headlines recently."

"I said, get out of my chair."

"And I imagine you would do just about anything to get back at Moe Dalitz for making a monkey out of you. That's why when I saw your ad in the newspaper, it occurred to me that you would probably be interested in something I have to sell."

"Sic him, Junior!"

The bulldog attacked, then hit the brakes as Zorren held out a dog treat he had taken from the desk. Scratched the dog's ears then stood up, introduced himself to Chandler and made his pitch. Describing in great detail how Lenny Circo was killed and how he had the murder gun with Moe Dalitz's fingerprints on it.

"Go back and tell Dalitz it didn't work."

"What didn't work?"

"He made me into a laughingstock in front of the press and after that put sand in the gas tanks of some of my cars. What more does that gangster think he has to gain by continuing to harass me? Doesn't he have some other way of getting his kicks?"

"Everything I told you is on the square, Mr. Chandler."

"Save it. I know that Dalitz sent you here."

"The last place that asshole sent me was the Ohio State Penitentiary where I got my mail for thirty years while he was out here in Las Vegas getting rich."

"Then why don't you sell him the gun?"

"I rotted for more than half my life in that cell for a murder Dalitz committed. I want money, sure, but I also want him to suffer for what he did to me." He looked seriously at Chandler. "Don't you want him to suffer for what he did to you?"

Chandler replayed the moment in that very office when a call girl sold him an improbable bill of goods that had turned out to be the real deal. Could the Lord once again be answering his prayers in a most unorthodox way?

"If you are who you say you are and everything you've told me is true, you won't mind waiting a few days until I can confirm your story. And if it checks out, I'll give you $5000 for the gun."

Zorren wanted a million.

Chandler knew what that gun meant if Zorren was telling the truth and after much haggling upped the ante to $100,000. A stalemate until the car dealer sweetened the deal with the keys to a 1963 palomar red Impala Super Sport with 195 horses under the hood.

CHAPTER 33

"Another middle finger to the Lord, Cliff?" asked Lieutenant R.P. Sampson as Chandler walked into his office holding a can of Coca-Cola.

"My faith in the Lord has never been stronger." He sat across the desk and took a long swallow of his Coke. "Have you ever tried this stuff, R.P.? It's delicious."

"It's also forbidden."

"Can you think of any logical reason why God would deny anyone the pleasure of a cold soft drink on a warm afternoon?"

"Because soda pop contains caffeine which is a violation of the Word of Wisdom."

"Meaning that God didn't tell people not to drink Coke, the church did."

"Which is the same thing."

"Open your eyes, R.P. Stop blindly obeying the arbitrary commands of an organization that is nothing more than a business making money in the name of God without the permission of God."

"That's ridiculous and you know it."

"The only difference between the Mormons and General Motors is that the church is not listed on the stock exchange."

"I'll pray for you, Cliff. But I won't allow you to sit here and disparage a religion that has provided my family not only with purpose but a plan for eternal salvation."

"And I'll pray for you, R.P. Hoping that you'll eventually come to your senses and figure out that what it all boils down to is that the Lord will watch over you as long as you live by the golden rule of treating others the way you want them to treat you."

"I have a lot of work to do, Cliff. Why are you here?"

Chandler told his friend about Ben Zorren. Outlined every detail of the Lenny Circo murder and of Moe Dalitz's fingerprints being on the gun.

"Is there nothing you won't do to try to get your hands on the Desert Inn? I know you don't like to lose, Cliff, but even you should be able to see that this Zorren character is trying to con you."

"That's why before I give him any money, I want you to check his police record. See if he really was with Dalitz in the Mayfield Road Gang. See if what he told me about the murder is true and, most importantly, see if there is a ballistics report still on file. And if it all checks out, I'll bring you the gun."

"I still say this guy is trying to con you."

"Then prove it by checking out his story. If it's all a lie you can arrest him for attempted extortion, but if he's telling the truth, do your duty and arrest Moe Dalitz for the murder of Lenny Circo."

"Okay, Cliff. I'll follow the evidence and arrest whoever is guilty whether you like the result or not. Everything done strictly by the book because I won't betray my oath as a police officer."

"That same oath makes it your sworn duty to arrest anyone who commits a crime no matter who that person is, correct?"

"Are you talking about a particular crime?"

"The rape of a high school girl."

"Is she over sixteen?"

"What does that have to do with anything?"

"Sixteen is the age of consent in Nevada, and if she's of that age any defense attorney will argue that the sex was consensual. Making rape hard to prove without physical evidence or a corroborating witness."

"I can tell you where to find photographic evidence that will prove guilt beyond any shadow of doubt, but that evidence could ruin the life of an innocent girl. Can you give me your word that you would do everything in your power to prevent those photographs from going public during the course of the investigation and trial?"

"I would never allow harm to come to any innocent person, so you have my word that I will do what's right."

"And will you do what's right and arrest the rapist even though he is a high-ranking member of the Mormon church?"

"Get out of here, Cliff!" Sampson rose to his feet, his face burning with rage. "I am not going to let you drag a good man's name through the mud because of some personal vendetta."

"That's not what this is about."

"One more word and I'll lock you up as a public nuisance."

"I report a crime and you're going to lock *me* up?"

"You haven't reported anything. Just veiled inuendo."

"It's the truth!"

"Don't lie to me, Cliff. This is just another one of your tricks to try to somehow get your hands on the Desert Inn."

"I swear on my daughter's life. Now give me your word that if I tell you where to find the evidence, you'll arrest Vernon White."

"You're serious about this, aren't you?"

"As a heart attack. Now tell me you'll arrest that pervert."

"If this is on the level, you have my word." The police lieutenant sat down. Picked up a pen and a legal pad. "Now give me the details."

"First things first. Get me the information on Ben Zorren, then I'll tell where to find the evidence that will prove White's guilt beyond a shadow of doubt."

"All right, Cliff. But I warn you not to take advantage of our friendship."

"I won't, R.P." said Chandler as he downed the rest of his Coke and tossed the empty can into the trash can beside the desk. "And thanks."

"Pick up that can and take it with you when you leave."

"Scared someone will see it?"

"Pick up the can, Cliff."

CHAPTER 34

Wearing a T-shirt and shorts over a yellow bikini, Charlotte walked into the executive offices of the Desert Inn and handed Harry's secretary an apple-cinnamon muffin, knowing that it was her favorite, to go with her morning coffee. Said she and Harry were going to spend the day at nearby Lake Mead and that he had asked her to pick up something from his desk. Then after a little girl talk, she was swiveling in her boyfriend's high-back leather chair.

It was the first time she had ever been on that side of the desk and picked up a framed photograph of young Harry with his parents in front of the Christmas tree at Rockefeller Center. Examined it closely, positive that she could see the sparkle of love in his mother's eye that Harry had described so intimately. Put it back in its place as the clock was ticking and she needed to get down to business, immediately striking gold as she pulled open the top drawer and saw a manila envelope with Bob Maheu's name printed on it.

The moment of truth. Betray the man she loved or allow Vernon White to destroy her family. An impossible choice that Charlotte knew was no choice at all.

She bent the clasp and opened the envelope, where she found several documents including an unsigned contract that called for Howard Hughes to pay $6 million for the purchase of a company called Allied Machine Parts. Gave the paperwork a quick perusal, put the envelope back in the drawer, said goodbye to the secretary then caught up with Harry in the coffee shop as the kitchen staff was packing a cooler for their day at the lake.

Under a brilliant unblemished sky, Harry piloted the hotel's cabin cruiser to a secluded cove where he dropped anchor then wasted no time undressing his girlfriend. Long legs and perfect tits. Captivating blue eyes and a flawless peaches and cream complexion he knew would freckle before the end of the day. They had sex on the deck, swam then had sex again. Nibbled at a charcuterie platter then took a nap, after which they did not feel the need to speak for more than an hour, content to hold hands and stare absently across the glassy water of the manmade lake.

On the way home, Harry put the top up as they drove in the direction of the setting sun. Taking the back way around the golf course as they got close, eventually pulling his Corvette into the driveway of a canary yellow house with sleek modern lines.

"Why are we stopping here?"

"You asked me to find out who lives in this house," Harry said as they walked up to the front door. "It turns out that you do."

He handed her the key.

She unlocked the door and was wowed by the magnificently furnished living room that opened up to a spacious patio and oval-shaped swimming pool.

"Am I dreaming, Harry?"

"I told you the day we met that things move fast in Vegas."

He took her on a tour of five bedrooms, four baths and recreation room with a wet bar and tournament-size pool table. Then Harry showed her the ultra-modern kitchen where earlier he had stocked the refrigerator. Popped the caps off a couple bottles of beer then returned to the living room, where Charlotte still could not believe what was happening. Then when Harry struck a match that ignited the logs in the stone fireplace and opened up to her about his childhood in New York, she finally began to believe.

He told her that he was an only child and how he and his parents had lived in an apartment on Central Park West. About family vacations to Miami Beach and how his father often took him to Yankee Stadium, always stopping first at the cigar store on Amsterdam Avenue to make a bet with Mister S. How after his parents died Mister S took him in and taught him that doing well in school was the best way to guarantee a future of which he could be proud. How much he loved Mister S, and was sure that she would love him too, when they met at a dinner he had arranged for the three of them on Saturday night. He told her how much he looked forward to coming home from work every night and taking her in his arms. To cookouts by the pool and decorating this beautiful home for the holidays. How her love would light the future and cleanse him of every wrong thing he had ever done.

Charlotte kissed him.

"I would bet everything I have that you've never done one wrong thing in your life."

"That's a conversation for another day."

She kissed him again.

"I know we've only known each other a short time, Charlotte, but my heart is bursting with so much love that there is no doubt I want to spend the rest of my life with you. I need to spend the rest of my life with you." He got down on one knee and handed her a three-carat diamond solitaire. "Charlotte Kaye. Will you marry me?"

Blue eyes with specks of silver were windows to a heart also bursting with a love that would be forever. Then Charlotte began to cry. Dropped the ring and ran out the front door.

CHAPTER 35

"The interim sheriff has started giving city cops access to the Strip in an effort begin the process of combining the departments," said Harry as he paced back and forth in front of Dalitz's desk. "And he's a Mormon elder, so we can forget about him ever playing ball."

"It won't matter once I get my hands on that TWA money."

"First things first, Moe. We can't make any moves as long as Vernon White is blackmailing you with Marie Taxitolo's letter."

"Quit worrying, Harry. That letter is as good as in my pocket."

Harry stopped pacing and looked uneasily at his boss.

"Please tell me you didn't kill White."

"I kidnapped his wife."

"And he'll get her back when you get the letter? Smart move."

"No lecture about finding a better way?"

"It's probably the only chance you have of getting it. Where are you holding her?"

"The Rogers have her stashed at the vacant Allied Machine

Parts warehouse."

"They didn't hurt her, did they?"

"She stays in one piece as long as I get the letter."

"What if after the trade we find out that White made copies?"

"He doesn't have the balls."

"Don't be so sure. We need a contingency plan that doesn't include killing him."

"A minute ago, you said putting the snatch on the old lady was a smart move."

"I'm trying to be the voice of reason. It's what you pay me for, so let me do my job."

"Your job is to do whatever the fuck I tell you to do."

"What if White refuses to make the trade?"

"Then I'll make him watch while I cut his dearly beloved into fish bait, then cram the pieces down his throat."

"And you still wouldn't have the letter. And even if you did have it, what if his lawyer has a copy? Or someone else with instructions to make it public in the event of his death. And what about Sam Giancana? Do you really want to risk an animal like him getting his hands on it? Because if he reads it, he'll cut *you* into fish bait."

"Who the fuck pissed in your Corn Flakes this morning?" Dalitz yelled at him. "Trouble with that broad of yours? She the reason you're being so argumentative?"

"Leave Charlotte out of this."

"Why get bent out of shape over one lousy broad when every showgirl on the Strip wants to suck your cock?"

"Knock it off, Moe."

"What the hell's so special about this one? Her pussy spit out gold coins?"

"I said that's enough."

"For fuck sake, Harry. It's not like you were going to marry the damn girl." Dalitz shifted gears. "And as for Giancana. If that greaseball even thinks about making a move he'll get it first."

"And then you'll kill the husbands of all the other women mentioned in the letter? Where does it end, Moe? If we're going to get our hands on Hughes's fortune, you're going to have to stop making gangster moves and start thinking like a businessman."

"I'll make all the fucking gangster moves I have to in order to keep White, Giancana or any other cocksucker from fouling up my plan."

"Use your head or else you'll be the one who fouls it up."

"*I* found out that TWA money is just sitting in the bank. *I* found a small-time crook who looked enough like Howard Hughes so that after a plastic surgeon made a few minor adjustments to his face nobody could tell him from the real McCoy. *I* taught him to walk and talk like Hughes until he was ready, then threw the real Hughes in a wood chipper and made the switch." Dalitz was on fire. "*I* did all that. Me! Moe Dalitz! And no greedy Mormon motherfucker is going to put the kibosh on something I worked so hard to set up just when it's about to pay off with more money than God himself can count."

"Then you have to be smart. Which means that you can't kill White."

"Nobody, and I mean *nobody*, fucks with Moe Dalitz and lives to talk about it. And if White tries to pull a fast one, I'm not going to just kill him, I'm going to torture that motherfucker until he begs the devil to take him," raged Dalitz as he pounded his fist on his desk then stood face to face with Harry. "Now get your ass out of here and fuck as many broads as it takes until you get your head screwed on straight. Then push through that Allied deal because I'm tired of waiting for my fucking money."

CHAPTER 36

Harry cooled his heels at the casino bar, troubled by the fact that Charlotte was not the only one who had pissed in his Corn Flakes that morning as a psychotic gangster was hell bent on involving him in a high stakes game of chicken. His eyes wandered about the casino focusing on nothing in particular, oblivious to the va-va-voom of twin redheads who eased up to the bar and sat down, one on each side of him.

"We're on our way to a pool party at Buddy Greco's. Change out of that business suit and come with us, Harry."

"I have work to do."

"What's the point of being the boss if you can't cut out once in a while and have some fun?"

"Maybe next time."

"Your loss, lover."

As the twins headed off in the direction of a good time, Harry remembered his own good time on the deck of the cabin cruiser. Fresh in his mind as if it had been yesterday, because it had been yesterday. Tried to shake the image but it wouldn't shake. Walked over to the bell desk and asked Freddy if he had seen Charlotte.

"Not since yesterday morning when you guys left for the lake. But I did just see Mr. Dalitz get into a car with two big men in light gray suits. Looked kind of hinky, like maybe he didn't want to go with them."

"Feds?"

"Not in that car. New Imperial. Dark blue with Utah plates."

Harry remembered noticing Vernon White's muscle at the Howard Cannon fundraiser and figured that Dalitz was on his way to trade the wife for the letter.

"Let me know if you see Charlotte. I'll be calling in for messages."

Harry thought about going to the movies. Maybe stopping by Greco's pad. Anywhere he might forget his problems for an afternoon. But instead, he gravitated to the Bali Hai where he found all of Charlotte's stuff gone as a maid was cleaning the empty room.

Twelve hours ago, he and Charlotte were madly in love. A story book romance. Had he scared her off by proposing too quickly? Nowhere to look for answers. Knew that she would not go back to Elkhorn. Maybe Hollywood? That was the original destination when she and her friend Barb had come out on the bus. No, he figured. She loved Vegas. But then again, until last night he thought that she loved him.

No forwarding address so he greased the palm of the desk clerk with instructions to call the Desert Inn if she showed up. Went to the house on the golf course but there was no sign that she had been there. Went to Lew's Luncheonette and sat in the booth by the window where he and Charlotte had first met, staring at a cheeseburger he did not have the appetite to eat. Thinking about how great she had looked in that white sweater and bell bottoms as they talked about Mickey Spillane and Dr. Seuss. How he had to convince her he wasn't a pimp before she would agree to have dinner with him. The beautiful girl with long straight hair so blond it was almost snow-white who evoked these memories had not just walked out on him, she had vanished from his life without even a goodbye. No message and no clue as to where she had gone. He replayed the proposal in his head again and again, but for the life of him could not figure out what he had said to chase her away.

He got a roll of dimes from Lew and called the desk clerk at every hotel and motel on or near the Strip. Thought about calling her friend Barb. But Barb who? With nowhere left to turn he called Information for the number of every Kaye listed in Elkhorn, Wisconsin. There were only two. He knew she had no living relatives, but maybe someone would know her. Dead end as no one at either number had ever heard of Charlotte Kaye. He called the Desert Inn operator for his messages. Nothing. Went to Churchill Downs and vented his frustration to Mister S.

"I feel for you, boychik. I really do," said the bald man through a cloud of cigar smoke. "I know how much she means to you, but did you ever think that maybe you didn't know Charlotte as well as you thought you did?"

Even when Harry was a kid, Mister S never came right out with it. Always softened the blow by letting him figure it out.

"What are you trying to say? Do you know something you're

not telling me?"

"You're not going to like it, Harry."

"Have you seen her? Do you know where she is? Come on, tell me."

"Let's go sit down." The older man led Harry to the race book side and found a couple empty seats in the back. "Charlotte told you she's from some small town in the midwest, right?"

"I've been calling there."

"You've been dialing the wrong area code."

"What are you talking about?"

"See the young guy over by the betting windows wearing a parking valet jacket? That's Ricky from the Sahara, a degenerate horse player who's in here every day. Says he saw you and Charlotte coming out of the Rickles show the other night."

Mister S waved Ricky over.

"What's up, Mister S?"

"Tell Harry what you told me about Charlotte Kaye."

"I went to high school with her."

"You're from Elkhorn?"

"Where the hell is that? We lived in Provo, Utah."

"You're confusing her with somebody else," Harry told him. "There are a lot of tall blondes in Vegas."

"She was on the pep squad and in some of my classes." Ricky checked the clock on the wall. "Only two minutes to post. Gotta get my bet down."

"He's wrong, Mister S. Charlotte had no reason to lie to me about something like that."

"Neither did he."

CHAPTER 37

"I don't believe there is a greater gastronomical pleasure than that of bacon," said Vernon White as he turned over several strips sizzling on the grill in the kitchen of a diner that had recently closed for remodeling. "Which makes it a shame, Morris, that your Jewish faith does not permit you to eat pork."

"I eat whatever the fuck I want."

"Including Marie Taxitolo, I presume. Which is why at this moment you find yourself at a disadvantage."

Tethered to the top of an eight-burner commercial stove, Dalitz strained against ropes that bound his hands to a gas pipe and feet to the handle of an oven door as formidable men in pearl-gray suits stood vigilant should he somehow find a way to free himself.

"Please accept my apology for eating while we talk," said White as he removed the bacon from the grill then put two slices of bread into the toaster. "But I cannot resist the allure of a simple bacon sandwich."

"Cut the bullshit, White. Give me the letter and I'll give you back your wife."

"No."

"Why the fuck not?"

"You are holding my wife, who I love dearly and want returned safely to me," White said as his toast popped up, buttering it then constructing his sandwich. Enjoyed a satisfying bite. Then another. "I, on the other hand, am in possession of two things that you want. Marie Taxitolo's letter and your freedom. So, as a matter of simple arithmetic, a two for one trade is not in my best interest."

"Make the trade or you'll never see your wife again."

"I'm told that the most common grievance among kitchen workers is the excessive heat."

"I mean it, White," snarled Dalitz as he continued to fight the ropes, knots tightening the more he struggled. "Turn me loose or I'll make you watch as I cut that bitch of yours into pieces then cram them down your throat."

White lit the outer gas jets to Dalitz's right and then to his left, framing his hostage with fire as he turned the burners up to maximum setting.

"Stay still and you will remain safe from the flames, although after a short while I imagine the heat will become oppressive, then overwhelming."

"There's a Hebrew word for men like you."

"What would that be, Morris?"

"Cunt."

White savored the final bite of his bacon sandwich.

Flanked by flame, Dalitz continued to struggle against the ropes.

White watched beads of sweat race down Dalitz's face and

splash onto his tie, then opened the refrigerator and poured himself a glass of milk.

"I find that there is nothing more refreshing after a sandwich than ice-cold milk. Though I must confess, Morris, that my earlier arithmetic was not totally accurate as you have something else that I want."

"You'll never get my hotel."

"First things first. Perhaps you can enlighten me as to why Howard Hughes is entering into an agreement to purchase the bankrupt Allied Machine Parts company for $6 million."

"Fucking Maheu," growled Dalitz, furious as it became obvious that ten grand a week was *not* enough to keep him from rocking the boat.

"My information did not come from Mr. Maheu, as he refused to violate the non-disclosure agreement he was made to sign by the man he believes to be Howard Hughes."

"He *is* Howard Hughes."

"You are tied to a burning stove, Morris. Do you honestly believe the best use of your energy is to perpetuate your tired Howard Hughes charade? I told you at the cemetery that it makes no difference to me who signs Mr. Hughes's name to contracts as long those documents are honored." White finished his milk then placed the empty glass in a sink of dirty dishwater. "My forensic accountant is in the process of unraveling the layers of Allied's hidden ownership, and I shall be less than surprised to discover when all of those layers are peeled away that the actual owner of Allied Machine Parts is you."

"I'm in the casino business. Why would I have anything to

do with some piece of shit parts company?"

"The only reason I can think of is that, even though both men are most assuredly deceased, you are exploiting the doppelganger Albert Lee Soames as part of an attempt to steal Mr. Hughes's fortune, and that prior to going after the bulk of his cash reserves you are using the relatively insignificant Allied deal as a test to see if your scheme will bear fruit."

"You're off your nut."

"In light of this new information, Morris, it would be shortsighted of me to enter into an agreement for only the Desert Inn when it's possible that you possess the key to a fortune."

CHAPTER 38

"Has Moe been around?" Harry asked Freddy, off-duty in jeans and a sport shirt as he chased a shot of tequila with a bottle of Schlitz at the casino bar.

"Haven't seen him since he drove off in that blue Imperial this morning."

Thoughts of Charlotte had left room for little else until a couple hours earlier when it finally occurred to Harry that if Dalitz had gone off to exchange Vernon White's wife for the letter, he would have been back long ago, making him certain something had gone wrong as his boss was nowhere to be found. Not at his office, his house or any of his usual haunts.

"Nothing urgent, Freddy, but I need to find Moe. Can you quietly put out the word that I'm looking for him? I'll be calling the operator for messages."

"Consider it done."

As Freddy got change and headed for a payphone, Harry fired up his Corvette and burned rubber down the Strip in the direction of the Allied warehouse. He knew that White had nothing to gain by harming Dalitz and figured he was being held as a hostage to be traded for his wife but, if that was the case, why hadn't he been contacted to make the exchange? He had been calling in for his messages all day, but not one word about Charlotte or about Dalitz.

The machine parts warehouse was at the end of a row of aging industrial buildings bordering the Union Pacific railroad tracks in North Las Vegas, and had not been operational for some time. Windowless. Layers of dust and for all intents and purposes empty, though the utilities were still turned on. And as Harry walked in, he saw the three Rogers playing cards in shirt sleeves and shoulder holsters, while Della White sat bound and blindfolded to a wooden chair in the center of the room.

"Untie her."

"Mr. Dalitz said to ..."

"NOW!"

After the blindfold was removed and the gray-haired woman in the prim blue dress adjusted her eyes to the light, Harry asked her if she was all right.

"I'm fine, young man," she said in a naturally pleasant voice as she rubbed the circulation back into her arms. "But could I please trouble you for a glass of water?"

Harry brought her a glass of water, then asked if she had been given anything to eat.

"I'm fine, really."

Harry glared at the Rogers.

"You haven't fed this woman all day?"

"Mr. Dalitz said ..."

"I don't care what Dalitz said. One of you go out and bring

this lady back something decent to eat." Then he looked at Mrs. White who sat calmly on the chair as if posing for a portrait. "You don't seem to be afraid. Why not?"

"I am in the Lord's hands. He will protect me."

"And I need you to help me so I can protect my boss."

"Would that be Moe Dalitz?"

"That's right. Do you know him?"

"I feel like I do the way Vernon complains about him all the time."

"Right now, your husband is holding him hostage to trade for your release. Do you know where he's taken him?"

"You seem like a nice young man. What's your name?"

"Harry. I'm Harry Lake, Mrs. White."

"And you may call me Della. But I am afraid, Harry, that I have no idea where my husband has taken Mr. Dalitz."

"Is there a phone number I can call to let him know that you're safe so that we can arrange to get Moe released and get you back home?"

"I am afraid I wouldn't know."

"Please, Della. There must be someone you can call and at least leave a message. At the temple? Maybe with one of the church elders? Who would you call if you had an accident or were in trouble?"

"Am I in trouble, Harry?"

"No, Della. But Moe is."

"Would you be so kind as to send one of those other men to my house to get my knitting basket?"

"Moe and your husband hate each other, and the longer this hostage situation goes on the more chance there is that one of them will be killed." Harry was not sure if Della was a ditzy old lady or if her cluelessness was a ploy to keep him off the scent, but either way she was his only lead and he kept pushing. "And you can prevent that from happening if you will just tell me how I can reach your husband."

"It's on the sofa in the living room. I'm making a red cardigan for Vernon's birthday, so please don't tell him because I want it to be a surprise."

CHAPTER 39

"You will see to it that my wife is safely returned home and that an iron-clad contract is drawn and signed selling me the Desert Inn, at which time you will be released," said Vernon White, knowing that, given Moe Dalitz's current predicament, it was an offer he was in no position to refuse. "Then once you have given me fifty percent of all monies received from your scheme to defraud Howard Hughes, I will hand over Marie Taxitolo's letter."

"My counter-offer is fuck you," said Dalitz, sweating bullets as the heat from the stove began to weaken him despite his best effort to remain steady.

"In that case I shall be left with no choice but to mail the letter to Sam Giancana."

"Don't try to bluff me, White. There's no way a greedy prick like you would willingly walk away from all this with bupkes."

"1147 Wenonah Avenue in Oak Park, Illinois is Mr. Giancana's address."

"Am I supposed to be impressed that you know how to use a phone book?" said Dalitz, sweat stinging his eyes as he continued to struggle against the ropes.

"I also know that Harry Lake has the Allied Machine Parts contract in the top drawer of his desk."

"You're talking out of your ass."

"Making it quite clear that he is brokering the sale on behalf of the actual owner, who Mr. Maheu has no idea is you."

"Did you rehearse this bullshit or are you making it up as you go along?"

"Mr. Lake is very ambitious. Will your ego not allow you to even consider the possibility that he has switched allegiance and sold you out?"

"He knows I'd kill him. Slow and painful."

"What about your own tolerance for pain, Morris?"

Dalitz spit sweat that had trickled into his mouth.

"It's obvious that you envision yourself as tough, but no matter how high your discomfort threshold, there is a point where your defenses will break down and leave you vulnerable to a pain so excruciating that you would rather die than endure it. And I shall very much enjoy discovering if your threshold for pain is as great as your ego imagines it to be." White gave a nod to the suits. "Begin at the bottom, gentlemen."

One of the pearl-gray suits removed Dalitz's left shoe and his sock. Held the foot steady while the other man took a pair of pliers and gripped the nail of his big toe and pulled.

A stabbing discomfort. Nothing Dalitz couldn't handle. Then as the nail began to loosen, the pain became unbearable, but Dalitz would not give White the satisfaction of letting it show. Gnashed his teeth to keep from screaming as the man with the pliers pulled harder and harder still until the nail was ripped from his toe.

"Are you now ready to accept my offer, Morris?"

"I'm going to gouge out your fucking eyeballs and use them for dice."

"In that case we shall remove another toenail. Then another and another until you agree to my terms."

CHAPTER 40

"You ate a club sandwich and I got you your knitting basket," said Harry, a sleeve of the red cardigan growing longer as he paced the floor of the empty warehouse. "Please, Della, tell me how to contact your husband."

"You worry too much, Harry. You need to have faith."

"I have faith in myself and things I can control, but without some help from you I don't see this ending well for anyone."

Every ten minutes since arriving at the warehouse, Harry had picked up the telephone on the dusty shipping desk and called the Desert Inn only to be told that he had received no messages. This time, however, he hit paydirt as Stiffy Woo had called to say that he knew where Dalitz was and wanted to meet right away at Colonel Cluck's all night fried chicken depot.

"Let's go," Harry called to the Rogers, instructing two of them to get in their car and follow him while telling the third to stay with Della. "Make sure she's comfortable and I'll call when we have Moe."

"At high speed it took only a matter of minutes for Harry

to lead Dalitz's muscle to Colonel Cluck's which was hopping with deep fried action. The colonel, a gray-bearded horn dog dressed like Napoleon, held out his hand to greet Harry then reported that he had not seen or heard from Stiffy Woo.

"Stiffy's not coming," said Hollywood as he pushed through the door and looked up at Harry.

"*You* left the message for me to meet Stiffy?"

"Would you have come if you knew it was me?"

"Where's Moe?"

"I don't know."

Harry grabbed the midget by the collar and slammed him against the wall.

"Your message said you know where Moe is."

"How about you spring for a basket of drumsticks first? I haven't had my dinner yet."

Harry looked at the colonel who was who was flirting with a busty princess of the night. "Okay if we cram this pint size piece of crap in your freezer?"

"Sure, Harry. Just push over the boxes of frozen shrimp to make room."

Harry nodded to one of the Rogers who cornered the midget.

"Stay away from me, you fucking gorilla," Hollywood yelled, then looked to Harry for help. "I DO know where Dalitz is."

"Why did you say you didn't?" Harry demanded.

"Because I don't, really."

"Freeze him."

"But I do know where the car is. Blue Imperial with Utah plates, right?"

"Where?"

"That kind of information isn't free, Harry."

"Where's the car?"

"I got expenses."

Harry peeled $500 off his roll and gave it to Hollywood.

"Don't insult me, Harry. If you put out the word to find Dalitz, he has to be worth a lot more than chump change."

"The car has to be close by or you wouldn't have brought me here. Now tell me where it is, or I'll chop off that movie star dick of yours and throw it in the fryer."

"Come on, Harry. I'm just tryin' to make a living."

"Have you seen anything odd around here today?" Harry asked the colonel. "Maybe well-dressed people on the street who normally wouldn't be in this neighborhood?"

"There's a boarded-up diner down the block and earlier I saw men in suits going in the back door."

"Big men? Gray suits?"

"That's them."

Harry snatched the $500 out of Hollywood's hand and gave it to Colonel Cluck, then picked up the midget and tossed him in the trash can.

CHAPTER 41

"Have you ever wondered why the good Lord gave men nipples?" asked Vernon White as he ripped open the front of Dalitz's sweat-soaked shirt. Turned on a battery-operated cattle prod then pressed the prongs to his hostage's chest.

Dalitz recoiled as an electric charge shot through him.

"Are you now ready to accept my terms?"

"Eat shit, faggot."

White increased the voltage, this time pressing harder.

"That's all you've got?"

White cranked the voltage up all the way and pressed it even harder against the nipple. As Dalitz's face contorted he pressed it still harder. Held it longer.

"MOTHER FUCKER!"

White pulled away the cattle prod and smiled.

"It seems I have discovered your threshold for pain."

"But you will never get my hotel or one cent of Hughes's money!" Dalitz yelled, the decibel level dissolving quickly as heat from the stove parlayed with the electricity coursing through his body proved too much. His head flopped forward.

"Wake up, Morris," White commanded as he slapped Dalitz hard across the face. Then slapped him again. "You will not be allowed one second of rest until we have a deal."

Dalitz tried to spit at him, but his head again fell. Then his body jolted to attention as White zapped the other nipple.

"What are you thinking about, Morris? Taking stock in your life? Your successes and regrets. What you might have done differently to delay your inevitable meeting with the devil.

"Are you wondering how many men your wife is sleeping with and if she has even noticed that you are missing? Do you suppose that all of the wives blackmailed into having sex with you will throw a party to celebrate your descent into hell? Ironic how you made such an impact on the lives of so many women when you do not care for women at all, only the power of sexual conquest. Not the sex itself, just the dominance to make them degrade themselves. Power gained throughout a lifetime of stepping on those weaker than yourself. But the time has not yet arrived for you to meet the man downstairs. You may wish you were dead, but you shall accept every ounce of torture I inflict until you agree to sell me the Desert Inn and divide all monies obtained from your scheme to defraud Howard Hughes."

With great effort Dalitz raised his head, but lacked the strength to mutter even a feeble *fuck you*.

Vernon White picked up the cattle prod and checked that it was still set at maximum voltage.

"Open your mouth, Morris."

The door crashed open as Harry and the two Rogers invaded the kitchen. Shots ringing out in both directions leaving one gray suit dead as White slipped into the dining room and unlocked the front door, pushing aside a sheet of plywood and disappearing into the night.

The remaining gray suit took cover behind a rack of canned goods, aiming his .45 caliber revolver at the Rogers who each held a gun on him. One against two. An impossible situation, as even if he shot one the other would definitely put him down. Would he surrender his weapon or would he fire, seeing it as a golden opportunity to sit as a martyr at the foot of God?

He chose option two and blew away one of the Rogers, then ducked return fire. Odds now even. Shots traded. The gray suit sensed movement behind him and turned as Harry clocked him full face with a frying pan. Stunned and bloodied, but still holding the gun, the gray suit fired in the direction of the remaining Roger, the bullet ricocheting off the side of the refrigerator and blowing his face apart. Harry kicked the gun from his grasp, scrambling on his hands and knees, getting to it first as the gray suit charged him. Harry aimed, and in a split second realized that when it came down to either you or the other guy there was not always time to figure out a smarter way. He squeezed the trigger. The gun was empty.

The gray suit pummeled Harry with his fists, then picked him up off the floor and slammed his head into the sink of dirty dishwater. Held him down. Harry holding his breath as tightly as he could, flailing arms and legs backward trying to make contact but all he made was a mess as water splashed all over the place. His final seconds ticking away with his head pinned to the bottom of the sink, Harry finally landed a kick that caused the gray suit to slip on some water that had splashed on the floor and fall forward, conking his head on the edge of the counter, leaving him momentarily stunned.

Harry gasped for air as he raised his head out of the sink then pushed down the lever on the toaster. Shoved the still-dazed gray suit's head into the water and slid the toaster in right after him, 120 volts jolting the thug awake just in time to die. Then Harry rushed to the stove and turned off the burners, grabbed a chef's knife and cut Dalitz loose. His boss drenched in sweat. Clothes singed and in tatters. Five bloody toes. Too weak to walk. Incoherent and unable to speak.

"It's me, Moe," Harry assured his boss. "You're safe."

Dalitz passed out in his arms.

CHAPTER 42

"What are you doing here?" snapped Vernon White, still shaken from his narrow escape as he arrived home to find Charlotte seated on his living room sofa.

"I came to tell you that I'm going somewhere so far away that you'll never find me."

"There is no such place."

"And that if you ever speak badly of me or do anything to harm my family in any way, I will come back and kill you."

"What brought about this hostility?"

"Las Vegas has a way of wising people up, and I'm just sorry it took me so long to realize that I have the courage to take control of my life."

"I control your life," White said, standing close and looking down at her. "You belong to me, and you always will because, as I told you before, ours is a bond that can never be broken."

"Screw you, old man. You've stolen my innocence, my self-respect and destroyed any chance for happiness with Harry. And now that I've made it clear what will happen if you go anywhere near my family, you don't have anything else to threaten me with. So, get it through your thick head once and for all that this perverted relationship is over, and you have no more control over me."

"Bravo, dear Charlotte, for summoning the courage it must have taken to say that, but unfortunately your words rang hollow."

"I meant everything I said."

Charlotte stood up to leave. White pushed her back down on the sofa.

"Threats mean nothing without the power to back them up. So, let there be no doubt in your mind that if you attempt to flee, I will be left with no alternative but to explain to your parents in great detail that their daughter is a whore who has betrayed the church."

"Then I'll talk to them first. And once I explain everything that you've done to me, they will understand."

"What they will understand is that because of you the family will be excommunicated, resulting in your father losing his job, your mother being ostracized in the community and your younger sisters expelled from school."

"Then I'll ruin my appearance, so you won't want me anymore."

"You can shave your head and gain fifty pounds and it won't alter the incredible sensation I feel when you wrap your warm mouth around my cock."

Defeated as he had called her bluff, Charlotte sank into the sofa cushions and visualized a future not worth living. Subservient to a monster. Trapped by his perversion with no power to stop it. Unable to even run away.

"Now get on your knees and do what you do best."

No choice but to obey. Sacrificing herself for her family, Charlotte got on her knees and lowered his zipper. Pulled out his already hard cock and took it in her mouth, suddenly realizing that she did have the power to end his vile hold over her once and for all by destroying his weapon of destruction.

Charlotte continued to go through the motions of oral intercourse as she had countless times before, questioning whether she had the nerve to bite off his cock. An easy yes when faced with the alternative of never being able to escape this monster, but she gagged at the thought of his blood in her mouth before arriving at the conclusion that it could not be any more disgusting than old man cum. Should she bite off the entire shaft or just the tip? Would her jaws be powerful enough to bite through the erect flesh or would it only partially sever, leaving her to chew it apart like a piece of taffy? What if she accidentally swallowed it? Tension building as she needed to act quickly before he ejaculated, and the opportunity was lost. She decided to go for the gold and bite the shaft. Was ready. Would never be more ready. Now. Right now. Her mouth gliding over his cock. Ready to bite down as hard as she could, but lost her nerve and jerked her head away.

"Don't stop!"

She grabbed his zipper and yanked it viciously upward.

The scream was deafening as White's cock was caught in the teeth of the zipper, leaving him unable to pull it down without ripping his already bloody flesh. He swung his fists at her, relentlessly lashing out through a pain so intense that it blinded him. Roaring as he stumbled after her toward the sweeping spiritual display that encompassed the room. But Charlotte was too quick, grabbing the centerpiece ivory carving of Jesus Christ and smashing it over his head. Again, and again and again. With each blow screaming "DIE, DIE, DIE" until Vernon White gasped his final breath.

CHAPTER 43

Bruises, contusions and a jaw that felt like it had been cracked with a hammer. A hot shower helped, but not much. Past noon as Harry pulled open the drapes and slipped into his black kimono, then as he walked into the living room to order up some breakfast a bullet whizzed past his head.

Harry dove for cover behind a high-backed chair. Snuck a peek across the room and saw Dalitz sitting on the sofa. Dressed to the nines with a bandaged left foot and a silver handled cane propped beside him. A .357 magnum in his hand.

"After everything I've done for you, why would you double cross me by spilling to Vernon White about the TWA money?" Dalitz washed down some pain pills with a swallow of scotch. "You're a dead man, Harry."

"I tore this town apart trying to find you, got the crap beaten out of me saving your life and rushed you to the emergency room where they took care of your foot and pumped you full of fluids. And for this I get shot at in my own living room and accused of selling you out to Vernon White? What the fuck is wrong with you?"

"That's the first time I've ever heard you use the word *fuck*. It's a tell, Harry. So, just admit what you did and maybe I won't kill you."

"You can't afford to kill me because you need me to sign Hughes's name on a stack of documents to get that TWA money."

"I'll find some other punk to do it."

"And he'll put the screws to you as soon as he figures out how much money is involved."

"Then I'll sign the papers myself."

"You're too close to this, Moe. It wouldn't take a handwriting expert ten seconds to figure out that you forged Hughes's signature."

Dalitz pulled back the hammer of the .357 magnum and aimed it at Harry.

"You're not going to fast talk your way out of this. I want to know why you sold me out."

"I need coffee. You want something?"

As Harry sat in the chair and picked up the phone to call room service, Dalitz shot it out of his hand.

"White all but said that he had you in this pocket. So, if you had second thoughts and killed him to keep me from finding out about the double cross you were too late."

"White's dead?"

Dalitz tossed the morning paper and Harry skimmed the front page.

"Nobody killed him. It says here that he had a heart attack while reading the Bible."

"My sources downtown say the Mormons used their juice with the coroner to cover up the fact that he was beaten to death with his dick out. So, to protect the church's squeaky-clean image he ruled it natural causes and quickly closed the book on it."

"What's the difference how it happened? I would think you'd be happy that he can no longer blackmail you."

"What doesn't make me happy is that the man I trusted with everything turned out to be a rat."

"Can't you see that White was playing you? Trying to drive a wedge between us." Harry rubbed his fingers to ease the sting of the telephone receiver being shot out of his hand. Lit a Lucky and flicked the match into an ashtray. "I've proven my loyalty every day for the past eight years and am well aware that there is no bigger jackpot than the one we are about to cash in on, so there was nothing Vernon White could have possibly offered to make me jeopardize that."

"Then how did he know about Hughes's deal to buy Allied Machine Parts and that you have the contract in the top drawer of your desk?"

"I did not tell White anything!"

"I had a lot of time to think tied to that fucking stove and, if you didn't tell him, there is only one other person close to the situation that it could possibly be. Your girlfriend."

"Charlotte doesn't know anything about any of this and she certainly doesn't know Vernon White."

"She used to babysit White's nieces and nephews for fuck sake. This broad shows up from Utah and cozies up to you in the middle of a power struggle with the Mormons, and you didn't think there was anything suspicious about it? I found out everything there is to know about that bitch this morning with just a few phone calls. She's a spy, Harry, and she played you for a sucker from the moment you met her."

Harry got up and looked out the window at the canary yellow house with the oval-shaped pool.

"Was she a virgin, Harry? Nice tight Mormon pussy must have felt good after all those skanks you fuck. Was that how she got you to think with your dick instead of your brain?"

"She didn't tell White anything because she doesn't know anything," Harry stated boldly, unsure if he was trying to convince Dalitz or himself.

"Just because she killed that asshole doesn't mean she wasn't feeding him information."

"First you accuse me of killing White and now you're saying that Charlotte did it?"

"His head was bashed in, and his dick was out. So, unless you turned homo it had to be the broad. The only thing I can't figure out is why. Not that it really matters because whatever the reason she can't be trusted." Dalitz raised his gun and leveled it at Harry. "And if you expect me to ever trust *you* again, you'll get rid of her."

"You can't be serious."

Harry ducked a shot that zipped past his ear.

"She's a loose end, Harry. And if you want to live to collect your fifteen percent of the Hughes jackpot, you'll prove your loyalty by putting a bullet in that bitch's head."

CHAPTER 44

"Get away from me, Harry!" Charlotte yelled as she picked up a fireplace poker.

"Not until you give me some answers."

She gripped the poker tightly. "Don't come one step closer."

"If you don't want me here, why did you leave a towel on a lounge chair by the pool that you knew I could see from my window?"

Charlotte raised the poker.

"Are you going to bash my head in like you did Vernon White?"

"GET OUT!" she screamed, hysterical as she swung the poker that flew out of her hand and smashed a floor to ceiling mirror. Ran down the hall to the recreation room where Harry cornered her behind the pool table.

The nine-ball sailed past his head, then he ducked a barrage of solids and stripes until she was out of ammo. Grabbed her by the shoulders and tried to calm her down.

"Who the hell are you to be mad at me?" Harry demanded. "You told me you were from Wisconsin when you were really

Vernon White's babysitter from Provo, Utah. You lied to me about everything from the moment we met. Played me for a sucker and almost got me killed."

"Let go of me," she snarled, struggling to free herself.

"You owe me the truth, Charlotte. About everything."

He released her from his grasp.

"Let it go, Harry. You'd only hate me more than you already do."

"Even after everything that's happened, I still can't bring myself to hate you."

"Shut up, Harry. A liar knows when she's being lied to."

"What could you possibly tell me that's worse than what I already know?"

Harry leaned against the pool table, waiting for an answer as she paced nervously back and forth.

"Promise not to hurt me?"

"I promise. Now tell me the whole story."

"It's ugly, Harry."

"I don't care. I want to know the truth about everything."

He led her back into the living room where they sat on the sofa, a lot of distance between them as she took several deep breaths to compose herself then hit him right between the eyes with the truth.

"The whole thing was a set up. Our meeting at Lew's. The Mickey Spillane book. He had done a lot of research and told me exactly what to do."

"Vernon White?"

"Yes. He said that instead of bringing religion to the natives in some Third World country, my Mormon mission was to spy on you and Moe Dalitz and gather information that would help him get control of the Desert Inn. He told me to please you sexually but keep my defenses up and not fall for you. Then when he found out I had, he was furious."

"So, you really did love me?"

Charlotte began to cry, clutching a sofa pillow as if it would protect her from Harry's reaction to what she would say next.

"He ... I can't even say his name ... raped me when I was thirteen and continued to do it whenever he felt like it. For ten years. Even last week. Even yesterday. Threatened to disgrace my family if I didn't keep having sex with him and spying on you. Is that truthful enough for you?"

"That's why you ran out of here when I proposed to you?"

"He was going to have my father fired from his job. I had to choose between you and my family."

"You should have told me. I would have understood the impossible position you were in, and we would have found some way out of it."

"There was no way out, Harry."

"Say his name."

"I haven't said it out loud in ten years."

"Saying it will be therapeutic."

"White." She choked on the word. "Vernon White. The pervert who said I belonged to him and that he would never stop molesting me, so I killed him. He's dead and I'm glad he's dead, but I'm scared that I'm going to go to prison. That's why I'm hiding here because I'm afraid to show my face at the bus station or the airport."

Harry smiled.

"What's so damn funny?"

"Because of the brutal and sexual nature of the killing the Mormons covered it up to make it seem like he died of a heart attack. You're in the clear."

"My fingerprints are on the ivory carving I used to bash his head in."

"The case is closed, Charlotte. And even if it wasn't, there were no witnesses and you've probably never been fingerprinted, so there is no way an investigation would ever point toward you."

"You're telling me the truth?"

"If you don't believe me, I'll go out and get you a newspaper."

Her smile built slowly.

Harry sat beside her. Tossed away the pillow and held her close until she finally believed she was safe.

"What about us, Harry? You say you understand, but will you still understand tomorrow? Next month? Next year? I'm a liar and a whore and eventually you're going to hate me."

He took her into his arms, and she pushed him away.

"And you wouldn't be human if you haven't already visualized the disgusting things I did with Vernon White, and those are images you will never be able to erase from your mind. Will the thought of me ..." Charlotte gagged on the words. "Will the thought of me touching that creep pop into your head every time you get mad at me for burning the pork chops or denting a fender? Will the thought of him violating me keep you from being able to make love to me?"

"The last time we sat on this sofa I told you that your love would cleanse away every wrong thing I have ever done." He brushed his lips against hers. "Now it's time to let my love cleanse you."

"That's a corny line, Harry."

"Not if it's true."

"And you actually think we can put all this ugliness behind us?"

"Absolutely."

"Convince me, Harry."

He kissed her until she believed him.

"As soon as I take care of a couple things it will be like none of this ever happened." He picked up the telephone and dialed. "Lieutenant Sampson, please."

Charlotte stiffened, then sunk back into the sofa cushions as he assured her with a smile.

"Lieutenant. How would you like to be promoted to captain?"

CHAPTER 45

"What's it going to take for you fucking Mormons to finally realize you lost and leave me alone?" Dalitz asked Cliff Chandler who had begun to feel quite at home sliding uninvited into the booth across from him at the Desert Inn coffee shop.

"I'm no longer affiliated with the church."

"You quit the Mormons? Bullshit." Dalitz looked across the table at the car dealer who was dressed up in a suede sports jacket and a colorful bolo tie. "What are you up to, cockroach?"

"Approaching the finish line of a journey set before me by the Lord that has delivered us both to this moment."

"I thought you didn't believe in God anymore."

"I very much believe in God, just not religion as a business. Any religion. I've come to see that they're all the same."

"You didn't bust in on my lunch just to tell me that." Dalitz chased a bite of his Reuben sandwich with a sip of coffee. "Just tell me what you want so I can finish eating without gagging on your rot gut cologne."

"Do you think Lenny Circo believed in God?"

"Who?"

"The man you murdered for the money from the Cuyahoga Loan Company robbery in 1937."

"I don't know what you're talking about."

"Then I'll spell it out for you. The police have the murder gun with your fingerprints still on it." Chandler pointed to the hostess stand where Harry Lake stood beside police Lieutenant R.P. Sampson and two sheriff's deputies. "Those officers are here to arrest you for Circo's murder, which means that while you are spending the rest of your life rotting in an Ohio prison cell, through proper channels I will put an end to the Howard Hughes charade and the sign out front will finally read *Cliff Chandler's Desert Inn.*"

Dalitz was stoic. No longer cocky and for the first time since forever not in control of a situation. Wondering how a thirty-year-old beef could materialize out of nowhere and bite him in the ass, then realizing that the man standing with the police, the one man in the world he trusted, had turned rat and set the whole thing up. He had no ace up his sleeve. No way out. The end of the line as he saw his entire life flash before him from his days as a punk on the streets of Cleveland to becoming exalted as the godfather of Las Vegas philanthropy, only to have it all crash down upon him like a ton of bricks.

"How does it feel to be squashed like a cockroach?" Chandler laughed as he motioned the officers over to the table.

Lieutenant Sampson held out his handcuffs, and Moe Dalitz was given the shock of his life when those cuffs were slapped on the wrists of Cliff Chandler.

"Stand up, Cliff. You are under arrest for murder."

"Get these cuffs off me!" Chandler yelled as all eyes in the restaurant focused on him. "You called me to meet you here because the fingerprints matched, and you were going to make an arrest. Not play a practical joke."

"The prints are a match, Cliff, but not to Mr. Dalitz. And the gun you gave me did not kill Lenny Circo. It killed Sid Klein and your fingerprints are on it."

"Why would I kill Klein? He was my witness."

"That's a question for the district attorney to answer."

"How can you do this to your best friend?"

"As your best friend I advise you not to say another word until you speak with an attorney."

Tourist cameras worked overtime as Cliff Chandler was dragged kicking and screaming from the coffee shop, an odds-on favorite to reprise his star turn on the front page.

"I told you he wasn't going to go away quietly," said Harry as he took Chandler's place across the table from Dalitz, who still could not believe what he had just witnessed. "Now do you believe I'm loyal to you?"

"Keep talking."

"Ben Zorren kept the Circo murder gun hidden away for thirty years while he was in prison, and he came here to blackmail you with it."

"The guy with the sideburns who's been hanging around the casino? I thought that mug looked familiar."

"That's right. I steered him into selling the .38 to Chandler, but what neither of them knew was that I had Zorren's girlfriend switch it for the .38 that killed Sid that I bought from the sheriff along with the location where the body could be found."

"Why would Ralph sell you the murder gun?"

"Because he was greedy. He kept evidence of everything dirty thing he ever did for you in case he needed to blackmail you with it later. That's why he was so cocky when he demanded more money. But he never counted on you getting him before he got you."

"How did you know Chandler's prints would be on the gun?"

"It was just luck that he was stupid enough to handle it, but I knew that just having the gun in his possession would be enough to tie him to Sid's murder."

"And the gun that killed Circo?"

"At the bottom of Lake Mead."

Dalitz signaled for the waitress to warm up his coffee.

"Why don't you seem happy, Moe? I got you off the hook for Circo, Zorren is history, Vernon White is dead and Chandler is on his way to jail."

"Everything except that loose end I told you to take care of."

"The problem with you is that your greed is greater than your conscience."

"You had better hope that yours is too if you want to see any of Hughes's TWA money."

"I won't hurt Charlotte."

"I believe now that you didn't tell her anything about our business, but I'm sure she overheard things and saw things that she added up for herself."

"I guarantee she hasn't."

"I don't care how tight that pussy is, she's a loose end. And if you won't put a bullet in that broad's head that makes *you* a loose end."

"I won't do it, Moe."

"Do the math, Harry. How much is fifteen percent of half a billion dollars?"

"Maybe you'll reconsider about Charlotte when I tell you that the Hughes deal is scheduled to close in the morning."

"About fucking time. You've been dragging your feet for weeks." Dalitz leaned closer. Dead serious. "But I'm not going to tell you again. That girl dies, or you die."

CHAPTER 46

Candlelight in the dining room of their new home. Beer in frosted glasses complimenting a square cut pie delivered from their favorite pizzeria. To Charlotte it was more romantic than their first date of lobster and champagne at the Sky Room. But she saw in Harry's eyes that his thoughts were elsewhere.

"It's not fair that only one of us is enjoying this."

"Life isn't always fair."

"That sounds ominous, Harry. Are you having second thoughts?"

"I can't afford second thoughts."

Harry stood then blew out the candles. Took Charlotte's hand and led her into the master bedroom. Slowly undressed her, taking his time as he savored every inch of her long perfect body. Worked his tongue between her legs until she let out a scream that rattled windows on the far side of Jupiter. Penetration. On top of her. Face to face. Lost in blue eyes with specks of silver that admitted him into her soul until he could no longer bear it. Rolled off so he could take her from behind. His hands rubbing her shoulders. Squeezing her neck.

CHAPTER 47

"Sorry I'm late," said Harry, a bit out of breath as he walked into Dalitz's office and sat across the desk. "Closing the deal took longer than I expected."

"It's done? You have the money?"

"I have the money."

"Then smile for crissakes, because now there's nothing to stop us from taking the rest of Hughes's TWA loot." Harry's expression gave Dalitz the feeling that he was holding something back. "There is nothing to stop us, right? You did take care of that loose end."

"I was wrong yesterday when I said that your greed is greater than your conscience. You don't have a conscience."

"Will you quit pissing and moaning about that broad? She had to go."

"You've obviously never been in love."

"I've been married three times, for fuck sake."

"Forget it, Moe." Harry fired up a Lucky. "A cheap gangster like you could never understand."

"Who the hell are you to talk to me like that? I gave you

everything. I've been like a father to you."

"I had a father. He took me to ballgames, took me fishing and made me feel like the most loved kid in New York. His name was ..."

"Charles Lake."

The ensuing silence had a sharp edge to it.

"You don't think I knew who you were eight years ago when you walked into this office and handed over that sixty grand? It had nothing to do with honesty or character, you came across with that cash to gain my trust in some misguided attempt at revenge for Charles and Patricia."

"I know what you did to her."

"I didn't kill your mother, I just fucked her a few times. Why she ate a bottle of pills I don't know, and I don't care. But what I could never understand was how you found out. You were just a little kid when all this happened. That's why I gave you a job, because I wanted to know."

"Sal Saperstein ran the cigar store book where my dad used to take me when he bet on the Yankees, a place frequented by larger-than-life gamblers who knew the score and gossiped like old women. Then later, when I ran away from the foster home Mister S took me in, and when I was old enough, he felt I deserved to know the truth about how my parents died. How it disgusted my mother to allow a creep like you to touch her, but she was scared to death of what you would do to my father if she said no, and how afterward neither of them could live with the shame you brought upon our family."

"From day one I kept a close eye on you, waiting for you to make your move, but you never did, because over time the hatred you felt toward me turned to loyalty."

"Only a fool would believe that a man whose family he destroyed would be loyal to him. I've planned for this moment since the day Mister S first told me about my parents' suicides. I got Big Paulie to give me a job that got me in the door and played you for a sucker every day for the past eight years."

"But you never made a move. Became addicted to the money and the lifestyle until you looked in the mirror one morning and saw that you were just like me."

"I'm nothing like you. You're cocky and predictable. You think that gangster pedigree makes you invincible but, without a gun in your hand, you're nothing but low hanging fruit too ignorant to plan more than one step ahead."

"Smart enough, though, that I'm about to get my hands on that TWA money."

"Remember all that empty desert land west of the city that you said was nothing but worthless rock and sand? I bought forty square miles of it from the Bureau of Land Management for peanuts, then turned around and sold it to Howard Hughes for $100 million in cash *and* the Desert Inn." Harry blew a perfect smoke ring. "That's the deal I closed this morning."

"You don't have the balls to double cross me."

"You double crossed yourself by keeping one degree of separation. Why do you think the Allied sale was taking so long? Because I made sure it was a non-starter, instead spending all that time putting through my desert land deal."

"Bullshit. Maheu controls every move Hughes makes and I control Maheu."

"Wrong, big shot. I control Maheu. And the beauty of all this is that you made it possible for me, through memos, to have Hughes make that crazy offer for my land. And since Hughes was already on record as wanting it, no one in his organization even questioned the deal."

Dalitz took his .357 magnum from the desk drawer.

"You'll never get away with it, you fucking piss ant!"

"I already have. I signed Hughes's name and my own name to a purchase agreement and the $100 million was wired into my bank account two hours ago. And the reason I was late getting here was because I was downtown submitting my gaming license application. Then when the commission approves my ownership of the D.I., I will have Hughes discharge Maheu with a fat severance package that will guarantee he rides off quietly into the sunset."

"I've got juice with the Gaming Commission, and I'll make sure you never get that approval."

"On what grounds? It's public record that you sold the hotel to Howard Hughes, so you have no standing."

"Hughes is dead."

"Because you killed him. And you can't trot out your ringer because you killed him too." Harry took a last drag then crushed out his cigarette. "Which means that you can't expose my fraud without exposing your own fraud, plus two murders."

Dalitz pointed the gun at Harry.

"I should have killed you the first day you walked into my casino."

"A smart man would have."

Dalitz squeezed the trigger six times. Six empty chambers.

Harry took the bullets from his jacket pocket.

"It works better with these."

"How the fuck?"

"My office is next door, and you never lock your desk. Like I said, Moe. You're predictable."

Relying heavily on his cane to hobble toward the bar, Dalitz poured himself a scotch.

"You had a long run, Moe, but it's over. The good life made you soft, and while you've been socializing with your respectable friends and kicking back at your villa in Acapulco the business has passed you by. So busy playing the big shot that you no longer are the big shot, with no idea what really goes on around here. Just like you had no idea that Ben Zorren was in town looking to blackmail you with the gun you used to kill Lenny Circo."

"And now that gun is at the bottom of the lake."

"Wrong. I have that gun, and your fingerprints are all over it."

"Seems I taught you too well," said Dalitz as he downed his scotch and poured another. "Every angle covered."

"All except how to erase the thought of what you did to my mother."

"Then kill me." Dalitz tossed him the gun. "Or don't you have the guts?"

"I'm not going to kill you for the same reason I kept Vernon White from killing you. The same reason I got rid of Chandler and Zorren. I wasn't going to let anyone rob me of the revenge I've been planning all these years. I'm going to enjoy watching you suffer, and for that to happen I had to make sure you were riding high so that it would hurt the most when I took this hotel away from you."

"Think you're pretty fucking smart, don't you?"

"Actually Moe, I got the idea from you when you were toying with Chandler. You said that the more you build up the ego of someone to let them think they have the upper hand, the more fun it is when you knock him down to size."

"Your mother wasn't even a good fuck."

Harry grabbed Dalitz's cane and broke it over his knee, then slammed the washed-up gangster hard against the bar and held the jagged wood to his throat.

"But she did like it in the ass."

Harry pushed until he drew blood then dropped the cane and backed off.

"Nice try, Dalitz, but you're not going to goad me into giving you an easy way out. I want you to live a very long time haunted by the memory of how I took the Desert Inn away from you." Harry fired up another cigarette. "And don't forget that the hotel owns the house you live in, so consider this an eviction notice that I want you out by the end of the week."

"You don't even know how to load the gun, do you punk?"

"You're going to discover very quickly that without the Desert Inn your society friends and your celebrity friends will have no more use for you." Harry cracked open the cylinder and inserted the six bullets. "And every time you see a TWA plane, it will tear you up inside thinking about that big pile of Hughes money I'm sitting on."

"What your mother liked most was when I pulled my cock

out of her ass and shot my load in her mouth."

A bullet exploded from the gun. Then another and another until it was empty.

"Not today, Moe," said Harry as he assessed the shattered bottles behind the bar. "There's a greater satisfaction in knowing that without this hotel, you'll be nothing but an old man feeding pigeons in the park trying to convince anyone who will listen what a big shot you used to be. But don't for one second forget that if you even try to make a move, the gun that killed Circo goes to the Cleveland police. Now get out of my hotel."

"It's *my* hotel!"

"I'm sure that's just what Wilbur Clark said when you kicked him to the curb." Harry opened the door. "Now get the hell out of here. I have a date with Angie Dickinson."

CHAPTER 48

Harry sat alone in the busy coffee shop, having a late breakfast as he gazed out the window of the bright open room and watched guests at his Desert Inn Hotel swimming and sunning during that in-between time when gamblers recharged their batteries before hitting the casino for another shot at money that would never belong to them.

"Enjoying the view, Mr. Lake?"

"I like what I see in here a lot better, Mrs. Lake," he smiled at the woman with hair so blond it was almost white as she slid into the booth beside him. The sparkle of love in her eyes and skin lightly bronzed from a Hawaiian honeymoon.

Charlotte flashed her wedding ring to Don Rickles as he passed by the booth.

"So, I guess the queer did read the manual."

She got up and hugged the man who was a head shorter.

"God, I love a tall broad. Treat her right, Harry, or this time I promise I will steal her away from you."

"Not on your life, funny man. I will do whatever it takes

to make sure that nothing gets in the way of us living happily ever after."

"Then you can start now," Charlotte told her new husband as Rickles continued on to his table. "Because if we're going to live on a golf course, we need to start playing golf. Finish your eggs and meet me at the pro shop. We have a tee time in half an hour."

As Harry watched his bride walk away, he felt as if he was the luckiest man in the world. Dalitz had been exiled, Vernon White was six feet under and the Gaming Commission had approved his purchase of the Desert Inn from Howard Hughes. He always knew that the flimsy murder frame he had hung on Cliff Chandler would never stick, but it had been enough to sour the car dealer on the casino business and keep him out of his hair for good. He was happy and relaxed, and as he polished off the last bite of his breakfast tried to remember the last time he had played golf.

"Good morning, Harry. May I join you?"

"Of course," he said, almost not recognizing Della White in a brightly colored dress that made her appear almost sporty and wondering what she could possibly want. "May I order you something?"

"A Sanka would be nice. Thank you."

Harry flagged a waitress then out of habit reached into his pocket for a cigarette, forgetting that he had quit smoking while he and Charlotte were in Hawaii.

"I'm sorry your husband never got to wear the sweater you were knitting. Please accept my condolences."

"You're very kind, Harry."

"So, what can I do for you this lovely morning?"

"I have something of Vernon's I believe you want. Marie Taxitolo's letter."

"That letter is an indictment of Moe Dalitz. And since he no longer has any involvement with the hotel or with myself, I'm afraid it's of no value to me," Harry said as he looked across the table and wondered if the recently widowed woman was in need of money. He liked Della White and wanted to help her. "Just out of curiosity, how much were you hoping to get for the letter?"

"$100 million."

Harry laughed. A cautious laugh.

As Della sipped her decaf, she marveled at the beauty and grandeur of the hotel, especially fascinated with the casino as she had never before been inside one. A sweet lady who chatted about the weather and the rising cost of yarn until she turned the conversation on its ear by telling Harry she was certain that it *would* be worth $100 million to him to cover up the fact that her late husband was Charlotte's father.

"This conversation is over."

"He impregnated her mother and rather than face the stigma of being unwed with a child, she married Robert Kaye and seven months later Charlotte was born."

"You need to leave."

"I have documentation including blood tests that prove your new bride was fathered by Vernon White."

"Blood tests can't confirm paternity."

"Charlotte and Vernon both have the rare blood type AB Positive. Robert Kaye's blood is O Negative."

"That still doesn't prove anything."

"I've known that girl since she was thirteen-years-old, and can tell you for a fact that if she thought there was even the slightest chance that Vernon White was her father it would destroy her."

"And to keep quiet you want $100 million. Every penny I got from the Hughes deal."

"Or else your wife will learn the truth."

There was no way Harry would allow anyone to hurt Charlotte, but he was not about to be strong armed.

"Do you really expect me to just hand over a fortune on your say so?"

"Perhaps this will convince you." Della reached into her purse and handed Harry a photograph. "Your wife with her father."

Harry looked at the graphic image of a very young Charlotte having sex with Vernon White. Placed it face down on the table.

"Who took this picture, Della?"

"I wouldn't know."

"Are there others?"

"Dozens of them."

"And you have no idea who the photographer was?"

"Why does it matter?"

"Because, Della ... the person who took all those pictures is just as responsible as your husband for raping Charlotte."

"I want the money, Harry."

"$100 million would make you one of the wealthiest women in the country. What could you possibly hope to buy with all that cash?"

"I'm fifty-one years old and never in my life have I had one thing that belonged to me. I was always the possession. Owned by Vernon and before that owned by my father. I was never blessed with children, so that money will give me the freedom to see, do and buy whatever the world has to offer without having to be responsible to anyone."

"You could do all that with a fraction of the money."

"For the first time in my life I have the opportunity to take something for myself and I want it all." Her tone softened as she looked across the table. "And if I am any judge of character, I think you will pay the full asking price to prevent the woman you love from suffering any more than she already has."

"I wasn't aware that excessive greed was a tenet of the Mormon faith."

"You know nothing about our faith with the exception of what can be easily ridiculed. If you did, you would understand that we Mormons take care of each other. To the point where if a woman is widowed, especially a woman never blessed with children, our community takes it upon itself to find her a new husband so that she will not be without family."

"Then let the new husband pick up the tab for you to see the world."

"There is no need for me to marry because I am not without family. Charlotte is my family."

"You can't be serious."

"She is my husband's daughter, and that makes me her step-mother."

"Not even on a technicality. Besides, Charlotte knows exactly what your involvement was throughout her years of abuse and would never have anything to do with you."

"I have faith that over time she will come to accept me."

"Forget it, Della. There is no way I will ever allow you anywhere near my wife."

Harry looked into the eyes of the woman who was alone for the first time in her life. No one to care for and no one to care for her. Grasping at the only thing that might make her whole.

"You never cared about the money, did you, Della? It was just a negotiating ploy to get what you really wanted. A quasi-daughter to fill the void in your life."

"Vernon and I shared everything, Harry. Which means that I know all about Albert Lee Soames, and the fraud you perpetrated to get not only the $100 million but this hotel."

"Even if that were true you could never prove it."

"This really is a magnificent hotel. I understand that before you moved into your new home you had a suite overlooking the golf course. Did you enjoy living there?"

"Very much."

"Then so will I."

"Not on your life."

"Vernon left me well provided for, and you're correct that I have no desire to take your money. But in exchange for keeping Charlotte's parentage secret, you will redecorate your former suite to suit my taste and allow me hospitality of the hotel so that I can be near my step-daughter for as long as I choose to live here."

"Do I have a choice?"

"Not unless you want your wife to learn the truth."

"What guarantee do I have that one day you won't change your mind and tell her everything?"

"I swear to God."

"Two conditions," Harry told her. "You immediately give me all documentation concerning my wife's birth as well as all sexually explicit photographs of her, including the negatives."

"And?"

Harry thought about his mother and decided that, exiled in Acapulco, Moe Dalitz was not suffering nearly enough.

"You send Marie Taxitolo's letter to Sam Giancana."

"Agreed."

They shook hands, and as she left the coffee shop Harry put a match to the photograph and watched it burn in the ashtray. Thought about Moe Dalitz who soon would have a target on his back, and realized that the psychotic gangster had been right about one thing. That sometimes violence is the only way, and that once Della kept her end of the bargain Harry would bring in a hitter from back east who would make sure that the woman who shared responsibility for raping his wife also share Vernon White's special corner in hell. His conscience clear as Della White would never again be able to hurt Charlotte.

Invigorated by the fresh desert air, Harry walked outside past hotel guests enjoying the pool during the in-between time when gamblers recharged their batteries before hitting the casino for another shot at money that would never belong to them. Past the tennis courts where he schmoozed a couple of VIPs, then on to the pro shop where he kissed his wife, knowing that she was right when she said that if they were going to live on a golf course, they needed to start playing golf.

THE END

ACKNOWLEDGEMENTS

Thanks, as always, to the great team of Sue Campbell, Allan Carter, and Scott Dickensheets for helping to making this book a reality. To Carolyn Uber for making everything a reality. To Geoff Schumacher for opening doors. To Dayvid Figler for insight and Ginger Bruner for a good eye. To Scott Seeley and Drew Cohen at the Writer's Block. To Maureen who will be forever missed. To the Gentlemen. To Jay and Star. To Ace Hogenson and Davey Klubs. And most importantly to my wife Katie for always having my back.

ABOUT THE AUTHOR

P Moss is an author whose novels and short stories offer a twisted view of life away from the spotlight. He is a musician and songwriter whose band Bloodcocks UK, the only American band never to play in America, have sold out seven wild tours of Japan. A film noir and pulp fiction enthusiast, he owns bars in Las Vegas and New York City and is an avid supporter of Scunthorpe United F.C. Learn more at pMoss.com.

Made in the USA
Coppell, TX
22 February 2023